Chicago:

August 28, 1968

Chicago:
August 28, 1968

a novel

Marilyn Levy

Montemayor Press
Montpelier, Vermont

For information contact:

Montemayor Press
P. O. Box 546, Montpelier, Vermont 05675
Web site: www.MontemayorPress.com

1 3 5 7 9 10 8 6 4 2

Library of Congress Cataloging-in-Publication Data

Levy, Marilyn.
  Chicago: August 28, 1968 / Marilyn Levy.
    pages ; cm
  ISBN 978-1-932727-16-6 (acid-free paper)
  1. Riots--Illinois--Chicago--Fiction. 2. Police--Illinois--Chicago--Fiction.
3. Vietnam War, 1961-1975--Protest movements--Illinois--Chicago--
Fiction. 4. Peace movements--Illinois--Chicago--Fiction. 5. Democratic
National Convention (1968 : Chicago, Ill.)--Fiction. 6. Chicago (Ill.)--Social
conditions--20th century--Fiction. I. Title.
  PS3612.E9373C48 2015
  813'.6--dc23
                              2015005875

For Larry who lit the flame,
then nurtured the fire

Chicago:

August 28, 1968

Chapter One

Civil Rites

I

Becky drifted out of the apartment on a wave of her mother's indifference. I said good-bye; I did my duty. Jesus Christ, "duty." She laughed at herself, quickly neutralizing her mother. Then dismissed her mother altogether as she ran down the three flights of stairs worn bald by anonymous feet.

Sprinting down Bosworth towards Howard Street, she caught sight of Violet, sitting in her wheelchair, her face digesting the intense rays of the sun. Violet liked to act tough. But she seemed sad to Becky, so Becky always stopped to talk to her. Even when she was in a hurry.

"Hey, Violet."

"Great day. Great day," Violet said, squinting at Becky. Becky was never sure if Violet could actually see her. A white eye patch covered one blue eye, and the other eye, enlarged by a thick smudged lens, kept changing direction.

They bantered about the weather for a few minutes. "Finally, got a breeze from across the lake. Made my own swimming pool from the humidity—sittin' in this chair. Can't wait till August's done with," Violet groused, before shifting to a graphic story about the changing neighborhood.

Nodding, Becky fidgeted with her sign. *What the hell? I can wait two more minutes.* Still, she had to calm every muscle in her body, straining to move on. She stared at Violet's wandering eye, trying to keep track of the story she was telling. She couldn't concentrate. *Just listen to her. Listen. She's stuck in this spot forever. Some day, I'll leave, and I won't look back,* Becky promised herself. Then, even though she didn't mean to, she grinned.

"Important day," Violet said. "Going downtown, I bet."

"How'd you know?"

Violet picked up her transistor radio and waved it at Becky. "I wasn't always sittin' in a wheelchair."

Becky felt a wash of shame flood her body and settle into her knees.

"I used to do what you're doing." Violet nodded at the Becky's sign. "Used to picket, used to carry signs like that. Ever hear about the sweat shops in New York?"

Becky wrinkled her forehead as if she were trying to retrieve a lost memory.

"Go kick ass for me."

Becky laughed; then she leaned down and kissed Violet on the little rivers of her age-spotted cheek. Which until that moment had always kind of revolted her.

Sitting on the El as it clattered away from Howard Street towards the Loop, Becky wondered why it had never occurred to her that Violet must have had a life before she got old and useless. It seemed as if Violet had always been old. *Like there was no history before I was born,* she thought with a start. *I guess I can imagine my father being my age. He's still sort of a kid. But my mom—she was always forty. Or a hundred. Why the hell did he marry her, anyway? She looked sexy—in those* pictures of her before I was born. I can't imagine her actually having sex. "Yuk," Becky said out loud.

She squirmed as a flash of embarrassment lit her face. Then she quickly stared out the window at laundry flapping at her from utility porches, as the El zipped past decaying apartment buildings in Uptown. She shut out the image of her father. *I was looking for something in a drawer of the knotty pine secretary—that was usually locked. Wow! Where did that thought come from? What was I looking for? Probably adoption papers to prove that that woman couldn't possibly have given birth to me.* Becky could see the box now—with a maroon velvet ribbon around it. *Must have found ten or fifteen anniversary poems my dad wrote.* She tried to recall one of them, but she couldn't. What she did recall were the feelings she'd had after reading all of them. Sad. Empty. Angry. He was almost begging for her love. It was pathetic. She shook her head to shake off the memory. There was a gap between what she knew and what she chose not to know about her parents. And she wanted to keep it that way.

By the time the El had shimmied underground and transformed into a subway, Becky had banished her childhood memories and was standing at attention in front of the automatic doors, ready to leap out the moment it screeched to a halt. Shaking from side to side, the train slowed, then jerked to a stop just long enough to disgorge a few passengers from each of the exits. She spun out the door and whirled through the turnstile, her slender, wiry body barely touching it. Avoiding the escalator, she took the concrete steps two at a time.

Carrying her anti-war poster, she cut through Sears, hardly noticing the vacuum cleaner salesmen lazily strolling among the merchandise. Then she crossed Wabash under the El tracks and entered the back door of the cavernous, multi-story building that houses Roosevelt University. She took the same route three times a week during fall and winter semesters. Now the nearly empty building felt a little strange and unfamiliar. Her footsteps echoed as she rushed through the back entrance and headed towards the front doors. I'm here; I'm here; I'm here, she repeated to the rhythm of her footsteps. She pushed open the front door facing Michigan Avenue. Across the street was her destination—Grant Park.

She shoved the revolving door with her right hand and quickly squeezed through the narrow opening, too impatient to wait for it to expand and allow her an easy exit.

For a moment, she thought about what had happened in Lincoln Park the night before. She saw cops chasing them, beating up anyone who crossed their path. For a moment, she felt scared again. But she forced the moment to pass, telling herself that the cops wouldn't bash heads in broad daylight.

Inching her way through the swarm already milling around the grassy areas, she noticed a group had congregated nearby. She edged closer. A black guy, dressed like some down-and-out preacher, was elevated on a scruffy wooden platform-like cart on wheels. The platform was tethered to a donkey. She couldn't hear exactly what he was saying, didn't know who he was, and didn't recognize anyone. But she didn't feel alone; she felt elated. I'm part of this, she kept saying to herself, as if she couldn't quite believe that she really was.

"Fuckin' A, man," the stranger standing next to her said. "The old guy might be a pacifist, but I ain't goin' down without a fight."

Becky turned to him. "Me neither. I hate the whole fucking establishment."

"Neat sign," the stranger said.

Becky nodded, pleased that he'd noticed. But at the same time, she heard her mother's voice. "You're always so contrary," her mother had murmured yesterday when Becky was working on the poster. Looking up from the sign, Becky had felt a momentary stab in her gut; then she'd shrugged it off and continued sloshing red paint on the 10x12 poster board that now spelled out MAKE LOVE, NOT WAR. "Always?" What the hell do I care what she says, anyway?

She was in Grant Park because she had to be. She could have told her mother that she was making the sign for Adam Bond, a kid she'd gone to high school with. A kid who'd died in Vietnam. But she didn't. I'm here for him, she told herself—and for the other kids in my class who won't ever come home again. She felt half-guilty; every nerve in her body tingled as the synapses in her brain snapped together. "I'd like to stick my sign in the faces of all those senators and congressmen who wouldn't send their own sons to Vietnam," she said to the stranger standing next to her.

"Or someplace even more appropriate."

Becky laughed at the thought. But it was the kind of laughter you hear when people tell funny stories after a funeral.

Becky had trained herself to stand up for what she believed in—much easier than standing up for herself.

"Who's the guy talking?" she asked the other demonstrator.

"Abernathy. Ralph Abernathy. He's some kind of minister."

Becky looked up at the Reverend and smiled. She'd brushed off religion years ago, but she felt calmed by his presence, anyway.

A familiar smell drifted past her. She glanced around. Then shifted towards the smoke. What is it about smells, she wondered. Danny's neck, she thought suddenly. She hadn't seen him in years. God, I dated him for months before I realized it was his Old Spice that turned me on. All that huffing and

7

puffing and anything-but-intercourse, and what I liked best was the smell on my skin afterward.

"Balkan Sobrine," she said. For a moment she wondered if she should initiate a flirtation. But only for a moment. Becky was intoxicated by the force of the demonstrators surrounding her. And her excitement was too strong to contain.

She stared directly at the guy smoking the pipe. She'd mastered the mess-with-me-at-your-own-peril look in order to ward off wolf-whistlers at construction sites and mumblers passing her on the street. But now, there was no hostility in her stare, just curiosity. He's older—maybe close to thirty. Doesn't look like the other protestors. Whoa—not even a flinch. Just smiling. The smile was a little disconcerting, but she kept staring, anyway. What's with the jacket? It's almost white—and linen? Probably plucked it off a hanger at Saks Fifth Avenue—a store she knew only from newspaper ads. Kind of cool, though, with the black shirt and black slacks. Also expensive. Balkan Sobrine's probably the only thing we have in common. Too bad because he's actually handsome in a sort of uptight Gary Cooper way.

The man drew on his Meerschaum pipe for a moment, seeming to use it more as a prop than as a source of satisfaction. "Want a puff?" he asked, offering her the stem.

She was beginning to feel almost giddy. "No thanks. I quit. But I still love the smell of it."

"Hmm, he said, putting the pipe back into his mouth and drawing in again.

She couldn't see his eyes behind the round, wire-rimmed sunglasses, but she knew he was staring at her. She took off her own sunglasses. The glare caused her pupils to retract to a pinpoint. She liked to surprise people with her unexpectedly deep green eyes shaped like a cat's.

"Been here long?"

"Not very." Lowering her poster, she ran her hand down her straight, thick black hair, parted in the middle.

"You from Chicago, or did you come in for the show?"

"Chicago, but I wouldn't exactly call it a show," she said, now irritated at herself for stopping to talk to an outsider.

He arched one eyebrow.

"Hey man, you don't have any idea what's coming down, do you?"

"Guess not."

"This isn't a freak show."

She put her sunglasses back on. "Gotta go."

"But I know what went down yesterday," he said, as she picked up her poster and started walking away.

"Oh yeah? What?" she asked, challenging him. At the same time, he scared her a little. Even the smart boys from her high school had looked like hoods and had spoken like truck drivers. And Roosevelt was a commuter college, where kids like her could work part time while taking classes.

This guy with his expensive clothes and wire-rimmed glasses looks like he went to some Ivy League school, she thought. She was both annoyed and intimidated.

"Is this a test?"

"Yeah."

"I saw a few heads busted, some people maced in Lincoln Park."

"You were there?"

"I live across the street from the park."

"Lucky you. Did you cross the street—or just watch us from your window?"

"Actually, I just watched from my window."

"Figured. Don't suppose you noticed the police chasing us all the way to Old Town," she said, trying to harness her

Westside Chicago accent. Despite her irritation, the smoker, she'd noted, was accentless. He spoke with perfectly formed vowels, unlike her and her friends whose broad "a" hurled up the backs of their throats and neighed out of their noses.

"Sorry I missed that."

"Yeah, I bet. What are you doing here, anyway?"

"Demonstrating."

"You mean watching the demonstrators. Or maybe spying on us. Why don't you take off that fancy jacket, lose the pipe, and pick up a sign, man? If you really want to demonstrate."

Taking off his sunglasses, he smiled at her, a half smile that invited speculation. She watched as he wiped his glasses against his jacket leaving a smudge on the sleeve. He tucked his pipe into his jacket pocket.

She was caught off guard by the intensity of his blue eyes that seemed to mock her. Then he squinted for a moment before replacing his glasses, putting his almost arrogant self-assurance in jeopardy.

"You a McGovern fan?" she asked.

"Not really."

"McCarthy?"

"By default. You?"

"Hardly."

"How come?"

"Not my idea of a candidate. Too white bread. Too bour-geois."

"Ah—you like 'em down and dirty like Nixon. You're a Republican in disguise."

"Nixon!" she spat out contemptuously. Then she closed her eyes. "I don't know. I'd have voted for Bobby Kennedy if I were twenty-one and could actually vote. Yeah, she said, sighing. "I would have voted for him, hands down. But since Bobby's gone, I'd write in Eldridge Cleaver's name."

"A rapist? The guy who hates 'honkies'?"

"People change."

"In that case, maybe I'll vote for Nixon," he said, grinning.

"Might as well. No difference between him and Humphrey."

"Nixon wins the election, you'll change your mind about that one," he said lightly.

"Maybe." Her attention drifted to the crowd beginning to spread out to the south.

He looked around, and then turned back to her. "So what do you think's gonna happen?"

"Don't know."

"You have no idea?" he asked, pressing her.

"I'm not one of the organizers, if that's what you mean." She studied him carefully. "You an undercover cop?"

"Do I look like one?"

"Kind of."

"Ah ha. No wonder I haven't been able to buy any grass."

"Here." She reached into her jeans pocket and pulled out a single joint. "Have a ball." She turned and worked her way into the crowd to get closer to the platform and hopefully locate her friends. The flirtation had run its course. At the same time, she was keenly aware that the guy was focused on her body. She wiggled her butt inconspicuously, incorporating the wiggle into her natural gate. Then she slipped through the crowd as deftly as a ballerina.

He laughed out loud. "Hey, green eyes," he called after her, but she'd already disappeared, leaving behind the smell of patchouli oil.

Trying to find someone she knew, Becky searched the faces of people walking towards her. Suddenly, a familiar tension caught her off-guard; the combination of fear and anger, gripped her stomach. She stumbled over an abandoned knapsack as she watched police, stuffed into their helmets and black boots, enter the park. Looking for trouble. Maybe aching for it, she thought. The air deflated. The party was over. She tried to analyze the situation as she bit the cuticle around her ringless finger. Just the sight of the pigs triggered her vulnerability.

She'd planned to meet Janet at noon. But Becky suddenly felt disoriented. The same people, who'd seemed like part of her community only a few moments ago, now seemed like strangers. Her heart thumped erratically, trying to escape from her body. Her eyes darted in every direction landing on Carol and Ray, two lawyers who worked at Legal Aid, where she worked part time typing briefs. Everybody loved Ray, a Teddy bear. Becky had seen him in court. He could also be a Grizzly. She tried to make her way over to them. But they got swallowed up in the crowd.

Finally, she spotted Janet, the only black person among the white demonstrators rolling along in front of her. The minute they were close enough to touch, she clasped her friend with relief. She was home free.

"Where's Richard?"

"Your boyfriend got a floor pass to the convention. I think he stole it."

"No shit?"

"No shit."

"Word of mouth is that the illustrious and noble Mayor Daley gave permission to meet at the Band Shell at noon."

"You're kidding."

"That's what I heard. One of the organizers got him to issue a temporary permit."

"Wow." Becky felt a little more optimistic. She checked her watch. "It's nearly noon. Let's go."

As they worked their way south, Becky spotted Staughton Lynd, her history professor, dressed as usual in a dark suit, white shirt, and tie. Hardly the look of a revolutionary. But he was. And he'd lost his job because of it. She noticed that the effects of battle fatigue were already evident in his posture and etched into the lines on his freckle-skinned face.

"We tried," he said.

"I'm sorry."

"I'm sorry, too, Becky. Suzanne Kaplan told me you lost your scholarship."

"Yeah. Never occurred to me that I might literally have to pay for my political activism."

"Ms. Kaplan got the boot, too," Janet said.

There was a long silence. Then, embarrassed by the weight of their failure, Becky and Lynd avoided looking at each other. She cleared her throat, once, twice, hoping to cough up some appropriate words. But she couldn't think of anything to say.

Luckily, someone at the Band Shell yelled into a megaphone, calling for everyone's attention. And guilty with relief, she and Janet made their excuses. Inching forward, they were caught up in the thrill of the moment. And she and Lynd lost sight of each other.

Becky and Janet got close enough to the Band Shell to hear David Dellinger speaking. "During the Tet Offensive the north Vietnamese raided the American Embassy, raided the Saigon airport, raided the presidential palace. We lost 1,000 soldiers in the first two weeks. South Vietnam lost 2,300. When are we..."

Suddenly, a popping noise startled her. Someone behind

Becky screamed in her ear. She turned quickly. Her motion frightened Janet. Shielding her face, Janet accidentally poked Becky in the eye with her elbow. Becky howled, unleashing yelps of pain that ignited the crowd. Within seconds, the police circled the whole area. They were closed in. Becky screamed with the other demonstrators. Out of fear. Not pain. "They're gonna smash our heads!" Shouting into the megaphone, David Dellinger told everyone to calm down. But no one was listening. In the commotion, Janet disappeared. Becky felt isolated. Her stomach roiled. Are they gonna Lincoln Park us?

Shaking, Becky leaned her poster against a tree. She held her hand over her injured eye. Tears streamed down her face. Then the police stepped back. The crowd relaxed. And Dellinger continued speaking.

"Need a tissue?" someone asked.

Becky turned. The guy with the pipe was leaning against the tree next to her.

Thankful to see someone she knew, her stomach began to settle down. But she didn't answer. As he looked at her eye, she wiped her face with her sleeve.

"What happened?"

"Got elbowed. My eye won't stop tearing."

He slid off his linen jacket and put it on the dusty ground next to the tree. "Sit down. Let me take a look at it."

"There's a couple of medics around here someplace," she said. But she sat down on his jacket anyway. The guy gently pried her eyelid open.

"Aren't you the little savior?" she asked. More from habit than from the desire to be cleverly sarcastic—her usual hedge against vulnerability.

"Not really the savior. Just Peter. It's all red."

"And?"

"And nothing. First you thought I was a cop. Now you think I'm a doctor. Just sit here for a minute and keep your eyes closed." He reached into his pocket, took out a clean handkerchief, and casually handed it to her.

She accepted it, smiling to herself. A handkerchief. "I don't want to miss anything," she said, intimidated by the handkerchief's fresh scent, a mixture of bleach and Tide.

"Don't worry I'll tell you what's going on."

A moment later, the crowd roared. Peter jumped up, straining to see why people were screaming.

"Maybe one of the speakers—oh, Christ—some long-haired kid is—he's climbing up a flagpole," Peter yelled.

Becky was disturbed by the lilt of amusement in his voice. She started to get up.

"Two demonstration marshals are heading towards him. They'll get him down."

"What?" she shouted above the roar.

"This guy . . ." he started to say. "Jesus Christ," he yelped. His voice an octave higher than normal. "It looks like the police are heading right for the kid. Wait! No. Not just for him. Oh shit. They're all over the place!"

Becky jumped up next to him, squinting as she uncovered her bad eye.

"I don't know what the hell's going on," he cried.

Police suddenly charged directly into the crowd. Seconds later, demonstrators closest to the cops streamed past Becky and Peter, trampling her anti-war poster, screaming, holding their heads, blood oozing through their fingers. There was no time to think. "We gotta get out of here," she screamed. As they careened away from the Band Shell, a policeman threw teargas into the crowd. The screaming exploded into hysteria.

Through a haze of tears, Becky glimpsed another policeman lob a canister directly at her and Peter. "Pig," she shouted. She automatically picked up the canister and angrily heaved it back at him. Shocked by the thrill of her own daring, she was barely aware of the consequences of her action. Other demonstrators heaved whatever they could get their hands on. Despite her blurred vision, she saw police rushing towards them. Oh no, I can't breathe. Choking, she tried to run. But terrified demonstrators squeezed against her. It was impossible to move. Finally the crowd, desperate to get out of the park, hurled Becky and Peter forward.

Panic, the fear of falling and being trampled to death, surged through Becky's stomach, burning her throat. She glanced at Peter and saw a look horror on his face. He grabbed her hand and tried to guide her across the park to a side street. Before they got very far, the police attacked from the opposite side. "We're never gonna get out of here," she yelled, her words gobbled up in the confusion. She felt as if her body were melting into a giant cauldron of cracked skulls and bleeding bodies.

"Just move—keep going," Peter yelled. But they were assaulted by popping sounds. Screams. Falling demonstrators stumbling in all directions. Bumping into them. Their eyes were smarting and streaming with tears. In the commotion, Becky dropped Peter's hand. She rubbed her eyes. Her sunglasses fell off her face. She looked down. They were on the ground. A moment later, someone on the run stepped on them. Smashing them into a dozen pieces. Her mind went blank; her thoughts replaced by the buzz of utter fear. In the midst of the chaos, she stood still for a moment. Then the sudden urge to pee galvanized her into action.

Still coughing from the teargas lingering in the air, she blindly searched for Peter. Damn, she thought, every time I cough, I have to pee. "Peter," she yelled, when she spotted him. She gripped his hand. "I don't think we can get out of the park. Let's head back to the Band Shell. It might be safer there."

They pressed forward. Through a haze of tears, Becky saw blood gush from the back of someone's head. He fell to the podium. She gasped. I wish I could make myself invisible, she thought. She flashed on an image of herself at eight or nine, waiting at the bus stop on dark winter nights when her mother was late to pick her up. I was cold and scared, so I made myself invisible. For a moment, she just stood there, as if she could make herself invisible now. She watched four demonstrators swoop up the guy who'd been wounded. Then the crowd erupted, bumping into her and Peter as they ran towards Michigan Avenue, screaming and yelling, as if they'd been caught up in a terrifying dance.

Becky and Peter ran with the other hysterical demonstrators. She screamed at the police, "Stop. Stop." Then heard the hollow sound of billy clubs and rifle butts. It nauseated her. Terrified her.

Shrieks and moans beat against her eardrums. The smell of blood and teargas filled her nostrils. Her eyes still burned. She could barely see as the police swarmed through the crowd. Killer bees, she thought. Not pigs. Fucking killer bees.

Just before crossing Michigan Avenue, Becky realized Peter wasn't behind her. She tried to turn back. But other demonstrators, pushing her towards the street, swept her along in their panic.

This can't be happening. It is. It is. Run. Her bladder pushed against her. Her head was spinning. She groaned from somewhere deep inside. And didn't even recognize that the sound had come from her.

II

Holding her legs together as tightly as she could, Becky stood in the otherwise empty elevator. Concentrating on the only thing on her mind at that moment—making it to the ladies room on the second floor of the university building. When she finally sat down in a stall, tears of relief came pouring out of her still-stinging eyes as she urinated.

She wiped herself and flushed the toilet. Then she vomited. Feeling wretched, she sat down on the cold floor waiting until her breathing mimicked normal. Once she stopped shaking, she got up and exited the stall she hadn't bothered to lock. So many boundaries had already been violated; it seemed senseless to protect her privacy now.

She washed out her eyes and mouth. But her eyes still burned. And the aftertaste of vomit still curdled in her mouth. It was familiar. She remembered throwing up almost every day when she was five or six. She quickly splashed water on her burning face and hair, dripping with sweat. Then she grabbed a passing glance at herself in the mirror. Her poked eye was turning black and blue. Her good eye flamed and was still tearing profusely. The tight curls she'd painstakingly ironed out that morning were again spiraling her head like a congregation of corkscrews. She was trembling, but she couldn't help laughing at herself. Jesus, she thought, I can't believe I actually took time to iron my hair on a day when people all around me were losing their heads.

She squinted, scrutinizing her face in the mirror as she tallied up her losses. Inspecting her wounds, she imagined blood streaming down her face. She shivered. None of it seemed real to her. Not the panic in the park or the pathetic unnecessary war.

Numbness began creeping over her, disconnecting her head and her gut. She could still hear screams of terror ringing in her ears. But they seemed distant. A kind of secondary chorus like ones in the Greek tragedies she'd studied in high school. And after all the screaming and chaos, the quiet of the cool bathroom seemed eerily unreal.

Like an automaton, she slowly moved her body to the corner of the room and slid down to the floor, her back pressed against the cold wall. An uninvited image from her childhood worked its way into consciousness. She saw herself sitting in the corner of the bathroom in her parents' apartment, counting the little white octagonal tiles on the floor. It was my safe place, the only room with a lock. The place where I could hide from my mother. What I wanted most, even when I was five or six, was a room of my own. Becky tried to shake off the image. But she couldn't shake off the memory of sitting on the cool tile of the bathroom floor planning her escape. She was still planning it. Now—impatient with all her fears—she bit down on a stray cuticle, tearing it away from her finger.

If someone were to tell her that one day she would receive the gift of another woman's child, and that that child would change her irrevocably, she wouldn't believe it. And if someone were to tell her that she would voluntarily sit in her mother's hospital room for weeks—then months, long after her father's memory—then his mind—then his body had betrayed him, she'd be surprised. But even now, sitting on the cold tile floor of the women's room, some little, barely recognizable part of her knew she was waiting and would always wait for her mother's longed-for epiphany, hoping for a sign.

It would come. Not as she would have wanted, perhaps, but before she lost consciousness, her mother would take her hand, maybe for the first time that she could remember, and whisper, "You're a good girl." And, that, in the end, would finally be enough.

"No," she said out loud. Her voice echoed through the empty stalls and bounced off the marble floor. "No," she said even louder.

She got up, glanced into the mirror again and started to smooth down her hair. Then catching herself, she stuck her tongue out at her reflection and marched out of the bathroom.

Her instinct was to head for the back door of Roosevelt. The safety and anonymity of the vacuum cleaner department at Sears called out to her. Instead, she got off the elevator and edged slowly toward the doors facing Michigan Avenue.

She weighed her options. I can still exit the front lines and hop a train to safety. For a moment, she felt relieved. No, I can't. Going AWOL is not an option. Lingering behind the revolving doors, she stared at passers-by, tracking the clouds of people drifting past as if she were watching a silent film out of focus. They blurred into one another, their clothes a jumble of muted colors.

Once she forced herself to walk outside the building, she realized that most of the demonstrators had left. She wondered whether she would find Janet, or whether Janet had taken the saner road. For a moment, she again considered leaving. Instead, she crossed the street and headed back towards the Band Shell. She could see that protestors had re-congregated there. Not as many as before. Maybe a couple hundred. It's almost dark, she thought suddenly. She began to panic again. Her whole body was electrified by fear.

She recognized Frank Reynolds, a TV reporter, standing in front of the Band Shell. It looked like he was interviewing protestors. Walking towards him, she decided—nothing's gonna happen to me if I stand next to a reporter. As she got closer, she heard chanting.

Who's the guy with the long beard leading the chant, she vaguely wondered as she approached the Band Shell. Then it dawned on her. Hey! Allen Ginsberg! she wanted to yell. That's what I want, she realized. I want to be famous, so people will listen to me.

Yeah, right. She checked out the fading crowd. You can't even get your mother to listen to you. No Janet. No Peter. No one she recognized. The churning in her stomach was gearing up again. As the sun went down, her short-lived sense of safety began to fade. But she was too tired to think. She just moved with the crowd heading back towards the street near the Hilton Hotel.

Standing on tiptoes, she nudged the girl next to her for answers. She could see that they had lined up behind the mules and wagons of the Poor People's Campaign. But she couldn't figure out why. Reverend Abernathy stood at the front of the cart, facing forward.

"What's going on?"

"We're walking to the Amphitheater."

"No way."

"Way."

"It must be five miles from here."

"Ten. Daley, the Great Umpa Lumpa himself, said the mule train could march to the convention."

Despite her fear, Becky started to giggle.

"You got it. As long as we're part of the mule train, there's nothing the pigs can do."

Becky flashed the girl a peace sign and retied her tennis shoes. She retrieved a rubber band from her pocket and pulled her hair back into the semblance of a ponytail. She felt almost triumphant as the procession began. With a renewed surge of hope and energy, she saluted Reverend Abernathy. He might not be Martin Luther King, but he's willing to give it all he has, she thought. At the same moment, she caught sight of Peter, looking disheveled. A range of unexplainable emotions sped through her. She quickly wound her way over to him. And started to put her hand on his arm. But she pulled back, startled by his blue eyes. He'd replaced the sunglasses with another pair of wire-rimmed glasses that magnified the tiny wrinkles around his eyes.

Just then, the light turned green. The Poor People's Campaign crossed onto Michigan Avenue. "Thought you only came for the show," she said.

Before he could answer, they were forced to stop walking. The light had turned red, separating them and most of the other demonstrators from the mule train that had already moved forward. "We're in trouble again," Becky mumbled, half-wishing she'd taken option one and gone home. Rippling with impatience, they waited for the light to change. When it did, the police stood in place, directly in front of them. The protestors couldn't move.

"Fucking pigs," someone in back of Becky shouted.

"Fucking commies," a policeman yelled back.

Then out of nowhere, Becky saw bottles and pieces of concrete fly through the air. And before she could figure out what was going on, some cops started rushing them.

"My God, they're going to attack again!" Peter shouted. He tore away from the other marchers, dragging Becky with him. Just as she began to protest, the barricade of police in front of them erupted. One cop paused. He stared at Peter for a moment. They had the same sad blue eyes. And except for the little scar that ran through his upper his lip, he looked so benign Becky almost begged him to help them. Suddenly, he swung his club at Peter and cursed. Before Becky could react, a second cop, his black eyes flashing, aimed directly at her. Oh my god, he's so close to me, I can see the hatred in his eyes. Instead of scaring her, it made her mad. She glared back at him, watching a bead of sweat trickle down his face. Then she felt a sharp blow on her head. In a blink everything began to whirl around her. She tried to force herself to stay on her feet as the buildings and trees spun around and around.

Staggering, but still semi-conscious, she refused to let go and fall to the ground until she felt the second blow. She tried to hold on. Then there was nothing. Blackness.

III

Becky could feel her heart thumping with an irregular beat as they drifted through the damp subway station. The burning pain in her head tortured her back to consciousness. Gradually, she realized that the violent thumping was coming from Peter's body, not hers.

She closed her eyes and grasped Peter's neck tightly as he carried her onto the first train that pulled into the station. Tears running down her cheeks weren't just from the teargas.

As the doors closed, she could feel the billy club pounding on her head again and again. Then she saw a horrific vision of Mayor Daley's wide-browed, pig-eyed, over-sized red face as he shouted, "Shoot to kill the arsonists. Shoot to maim the looters."

Seated in the sanctuary of the almost empty car, Becky tried to stop the pain beating against her head. She put her hand on the spot that hurt most and felt blood. She found a second spot where blood was gushing out. She whimpered, afraid her head would explode.

The speeding train jerked from side to side, making the pain worse. Peter's arm was wrapped around her shoulders. He held her tightly against his side. She could still feel his uneven breathing and wondered if he'd been hurt. She tried to ask. She wanted to reassure him that she was all right, though she wasn't, but her head was spinning; she couldn't locate the words.

"I'm taking you to the emergency room at Northwestern Hospital," he said. She wanted to argue with him, but she didn't. She forced herself to speak. "You okay?" she finally asked. With some difficulty, she turned towards him and noted patches of blood on his shirt and sprinkles of blood on his face. They looked like uneven freckles. The actual sound of her voice made her feel a little better.

"It's yours. And maybe someone else's. They missed me. Almost. Took one hit to the shoulder."

"Lucky you," she mumbled.

"Yeah. Lucky me. We're getting off at the next stop."

They sat in the emergency room for an hour before the attending physician shaved off patches of her hair and sewed up her head—in two different places. By that time blood had poured out of her head onto her face and clothes. The smell and the pain made her even dizzier and more nauseated.

"Could have been worse," the attending said to Peter, as if she weren't in the room. He planted a bandage across her forehead and shaved head.

She still felt disoriented when they left the hospital. But she didn't want to go home. She didn't want go any place where people would ask her questions she didn't want to answer. "Didn't you say you live across from Lincoln Park?"

"Yeah."

"I—can I just rest at your place for a little while before I go home?"

Peter hesitated; then shrugged his shoulders. "Sure. We can grab a cab and be there in five minutes."

"I'm sorry," she said, as they got out of the cab and walked towards his apartment.

"For what?"

"I still feel kind of shaky."

"Me, too," he admitted. He squeezed her fingers gently.

"If you hadn't been there . . ."

"Pretty barbaric initiation for a first date," he said. As if he needed to brush off any taint of sentimentality.

She hesitated for a moment, reaching for a comeback. "Yeah," she finally answered without much enthusiasm. It seemed sacrilegious to play games on the bones of battered demonstrators.

They reached his apartment and hiked up three flights of stairs. "Hold on," he said after they entered. "I'll grab a clean shirt for you."

A minute later, he came out of his bedroom carrying a freshly ironed blue shirt with a buttoned-down collar. "Why don't you go wash up? "Bathroom's over there."

She felt wobbly and didn't trust herself to stand. Gingerly, she leaned against the sink and stood in front of the mirror staring at her pale face. She was afraid she'd faint if she leaned over. She reached down slowly, grabbed a hand full of tissues, wet them. And then washed her face and hands. She glanced at a clean towel on the towel rack; then grabbed more tissues to dry herself. Safe and not safe, she thought. She started to slowly unbutton her shirt. Then she ripped it off and threw it into a wastepaper basket.

Peter, too, had taken off his black shirt was now wearing a clean blue and white stripped shirt as he led her into the kitchen. She moved quietly towards his scarred oak table, looking and feeling very fragile in his heavily-starched shirt that hung down to her knees. Walking up the steps had exhausted her.

It was only after she sat down that they both realized they hadn't eaten all day.

"Let's see what's in here," Peter said. He scrounged around in the refrigerator. Then pulled out a couple of beers. He searched for something to eat, settling on a carton of eggs, two English muffins, and a small jar of what looked to Becky like little black beads.

Becky felt comforted by the steadiness of the ritual as she watched him break the eggs, one by one. She concentrated on his hand as he whipped the eggs with a fork until they were foamy. His fingers are long and thin, delicate, almost like a woman's, she thought. Or a pianist's. Or maybe a basketball player's. She started to breathe normally, allowing her breath to reach beyond the confines of her chest. I'm safe, she thought. At least, for the moment.

By the time their impromptu dinner was ready, Peter had drunk half the beer. He slipped into a chair across from Becky, raised his bottle to his lips and finished the rest of the beer without putting it down again. Becky wanted to raise her bottle to her mouth and join him, but she wasn't sure she could lift her arm. Her eyes no longer burned from the teargas, but everything around her still seemed slightly unfocused. I feel like I'm looking at him through somebody else's eyes, the eyes of someone who belongs here. Staccato thoughts sprinted through her head, almost as if they were coming from disconnected parts of her brain. I made him bring me here. I should have gone home. He doesn't want me to be here. He's completely calm. Sitting here drinking his beer. I'm a wreck. I have to leave. I can't leave.

She was surprised to find some bodiless hand lifting her own bottle to her lips. She drank slowly, feeling warmth spread out and make its way into her stomach and her head at the same time, easing away the exhaustion and the headache. By sheer will power, she removed the filter from her lens. Little by little, everything gradually became clearer. She looked at Peter's face. He was smiling at her, not without some irony, she thought. Now that they were alone, she felt awkward and out of her element. As he spooned the tiny black caviar beads onto their eggs, he seemed to disappear inside himself. He smiled at her again, but she sensed that he was smiling at her from a distance. See me, she prayed. She watched his hand carry his fork back and forth from his plate to his mouth in an almost hypnotic rhythm. Love me, she wished before she could censor herself with her mother's favorite saying, "If wishes were horses, beggars would ride."

Finally, she picked up her own fork and began eating the offering he'd placed in front of her. The sharp, salty, unfamiliar taste of caviar worried her tongue. She wanted to spit it out. Instead, she allowed it to slide down her throat.

The gentle clinking of forks on their plates filled the space between them. She was acutely aware of every little sound. She knew he was too. What's he thinking? What's he feeling? He probably wishes he'd never met me. She tried to hold herself straight-backed in her chair.

"You look around, and you see it happening to other people," she said nervously, "but you're still okay, so it doesn't seem real. It's not real until it happens to you."

"It was real enough for me. Want anything else?" he asked politely. But he didn't look at her. He stared at his hands.

What would it feel like if he touched me? "No thanks," she answered, politely.

Then he cocked his head and smiled at her. And again, she noticed the tiny lines around his eyes and wondered if they somehow told more of his story than he intended to reveal. She got up from the table and switched on the radio. She moved the dial back and forth trying to catch the news. It was twenty minutes to the hour, so there were only music and religious programs. "It's like the rest of the city has no idea about what happened today." She turned off the radio.

"TV's in the living room. Why don't you go in and turn it on? Maybe you can catch some news there. I'll clean up in here," he said.

She slipped out of the kitchen as he cleared the table. I should go home, she thought again. She put her hand in her pocket and probed for the three dollars she'd stuffed in there that morning. But the thought of facing my mother makes my head ache even worse. She eyed the phone in the living room, picked it up and dialed Janet's number. She wasn't surprised when no one answered. I should call Richard. He's probably worrying about me. He's probably still at the Amphitheater. And what would I tell him, anyway?

She tentatively walked into the living room and glanced around at the sparse furniture: a creased, overstuffed brown leather couch with a matching chair, a couple of metal lamps sporting glass shades on which delicate flowers were separated by thin black metal strips, and a large fringed rug with a repeated pattern of faded reds and blues. She figured it was all second hand and wondered why a guy like Peter would decorate a room with used stuff. She also momentarily wondered what kind of guy had flowered lampshades.

Sitting down on the floor directly in front of the TV, she punched on Channel 2, WBBM, and waited impatiently for the screen to fill up. Finally, the images burst out at her in color. Involuntarily, she reached up to touch the bandage on her forehead as she watched the wave of blue uniforms wash over the crowd.

She was overcome by an incredible mix of emotions; anger at the betrayal, sadness because of the useless pain, and elation. She watched the police clubbing innocent people who weren't even part of the demonstration, and she realized that everyone sitting in front of a television set was also watching.

She turned up the sound.

"An estimated 10,000 anti-war protesters filled the streets of Chicago today," Walter Cronkite announced. Look at him. He's shocked, she thought. This is good. This is great. The whole country will see what the fucking pigs did.

Becky turned the TV up still louder until the sounds of the civil war totally surrounded her.

"Police and National Guardsmen called out to vanquish the demonstrators, only increased the tension," Cronkite continued before he cut to a re-run of Frank Reynolds, reporting from the field. Above the chaos, Reynolds breathlessly yelled, "The police are attacking the demonstrators with clubs and rifle butts and teargas."

Becky held her breath. She watched Reynolds and his cameraman run along with the demonstrators, the camera jerking.

From the safety of the newsroom, Walter Cronkite reported that hundreds of demonstrators had been arrested.

"We won," she yelled. Her eyes blazing with excitement.

"Not what it looks like to me," Peter said, as he walked into the room.

"Listen. Listen to them," she said, switching to Channel 7. Then Channel 4. "It's on every channel."

Suddenly, Channel 4 cut to footage of Dan Rather, knocked to the floor of the Convention Center. Security guards were dragging him from the hall.

On Channel 2, they saw demonstrators chanting, "The whole world is watching. The whole world is watching you."

"Maybe we lost the battle, but we haven't lost the fucking war! They have to listen to us now," Becky screamed, her fist raised in the air, her headache and confusion momentarily forgotten. This was real. This was something she understood. It would be many years before she understood just how real it had been.

"'They?'"

Peter settled his long body on the floor beside her, almost dwarfing her. With her unruly hair, wearing Peter's oversized shirt, Becky looked like a wild child by comparison.

"They— They—everyone who isn't us. The slugs at the Amphitheater," she answered, without taking her eyes from the screen.

He smiled. "I don't think they're watching TV. The whole world might be tuned into what's going on here, but I don't think the delegates down at the Amphitheater really give a damn. Not in this election, anyway. Humphrey walks off with the nomination regardless of the number of broken heads."

"That's cynical." She was pained by his cynicism. She wanted to convert him to her faith. Turning from the TV and looking directly into his eyes, she tried to draw him in. If he believed in her cause, he might believe in her. "We're sending the government a message here. We're making history!"

He reached over and lightly touched her hair. I want to kiss his hand, she thought.

"How's the head?"

"Okay."

The continuous news coverage filled the space between them.

She was aware of her own breathing and his. She smelled the blood and the raw, familiar, almost bitter mixture, coming from both their bodies.

The only real light in the room burst out of the TV, creating a strobe-like effect, dizzying her again.

She'd inadvertently neglected to button his shirt all the way up. The top three remained free, so the shirt gapped when she leaned forward, exposing her chest. "Blood," he said. He skirted her small breasts with one finger, tracing the splatters of blood that had seeped through her work shirt and flowered in Jackson Pollack-like splashes all over her body.

She breathed in his hair and his body, sweet and sour and sensual. And ached for the moment to be more than it was.

"We gotta get you home."

He kissed the tip of her nose; then he reached out his hands and helped her to her feet. Again, she looked into his eyes and thought she saw a hidden promise.

For a moment, she felt giddy with fear, excitement and possibility. Peter leaned towards her.

He smiled a bit nervously and led her to the door.

"It's been a long day," he said.

She glanced back at the TV still blaring. Then quickly took in the rest of the room. As if she might need to remember it some day.

Chapter Two

Peter and the Wolves

I

As they walked down the stairs of his apartment building, Peter offered to drive Becky home.

"Hey," she said, "I'm a big girl. I don't need anyone to deposit me at my door."

"At least, let me ride the El with you."

"After all we've gone through today, taking the El to Howard Street and walking two blocks to my apartment isn't exactly threatening."

Relieved, he walked her to the train station and then headed back towards the luxurious emptiness of his own apartment, hoping to reclaim his life. Never asked her last name. Maybe I should've invited her to spend the night. Thought about it. Wanted to. Glad I sidestepped the temptation. Already shared too much of ourselves—or maybe too little. The whole fucking day turned into a nightmare.

But as he made his way home, Peter felt empty. He glanced at his watch. Maybe I'll call Tom. See what his take on the whole mess is. His chest tightened. He felt the square of tension shift into place. He tried to ignore it—breathe past it, relegating the events of the day into the distance, so they seemed slightly unreal—like the rest of my life—he thought with some irony.

Peter had walked out of the School of the Art Institute on Michigan Avenue at 11:00 o'clock that morning, wondering why he'd agreed to teach a painting class in summer school. His students were only eight or ten years younger, but they belonged to a totally different generation. I understand some of their attitudes, he mused. But I object to the blatantly graphic way they thumb their noses at established art. At the establishment in general. Still, they value my opinion—or pretend to—even when I don't feel like giving it. He sighed. In a way, I envy their ability to live in the present, as they say. Brag about living in the present would be more like it. But they think history—personal and political—is totally insignificant. The past only a jumping off point from which to confront tradition and piss on it. He laughed to himself. Maybe they're right. At least about personal history.

Breathing more easily after escaping the classroom, he decided to keep walking south to Grant Park. Why not, he thought. In the past few days an electric energy replaced the collective sweat that had hung from Chicago's lamp posts all summer and had draped the Hancock Building and the Marina Towers like a gauze shroud. The walk'll do me good. I can check out the anti-war demonstration. Maybe find Tom.

Too bad about Bobby Kennedy. Too damn bad. Now there was a guy I could admire. But poor old Humphrey, he mused, as he picked up his pace. The guy just isn't Bobby Kennedy. And neither is McCarthy or crazies like Hoffman and Rubin.

Thinking about Hoffman and Rubin reminded him of the night before. From the window of his apartment, Peter had had a clear view of the chaos in Lincoln Park. Jesus, it was like a fucking Brueghel painting. The police chasing hippies in all directions. Hoffman and his band of Yippies serving up their anti-war antics in a pot of Halloween stew. He was mildly curious about whether the carnival would continue in Grant

Park but didn't think there would be any problems. Nothing's going to happen while it's still light, Peter decided. So he sauntered into Grant Park. Always reminds me of "A Sunday Afternoon on the Island of La Grande Jatte." Families picnicking. Kids gyrating with hoola hoops.

Hundreds of people were milling around the area across the street from the Hilton Hotel where most of the delegates were staying. Peter's father had gone to Yale with one of the delegates from Maine—or was it New Hampshire? For a moment, he wondered if he'd run into the old man. That made him laugh.

Before moving towards the crowd, he took out his pipe, his tamper, and his tobacco, squinting as he scanned the area looking for someone interesting to talk to. Interesting to him was female, beautiful, and clean. He played basketball at least twice a week and ran every day, so was in good shape. Though that wasn't the object of his exercise. It was more about working off excess energy so he could keep focused. Keep calm, maybe. But to his surprise, his students—male and female—women he randomly met at parties, even the wives of friends—all but threw themselves at him.

He thought about the woman with great tits who'd sidled up to him at a dinner party. Every other guy there had tried to corner her. Still remember the smell of her body oil.

"Your indifference turns me on," she said.

Laughed. Spoiled the whole seduction. Gorgeous women out there looking for love—or the closest facsimile. No commitments on either side. Suits my temperament.

When he finished fiddling with his pipe, Peter noticed a middle-aged, rather heavy-set black man in dark clothes, looking distinctly out of place. He seemed to be addressing the people around him from a make-shift platform on wheels.

"Who's that? Who's that?" rippled through the crowd. No one standing near Peter seemed to know.

Despite the fact that he couldn't be heard very well, the speaker continued. The crowd pushed in closer. Peter could catch about every third word and finally figured out that the man on the platform was the leader of something called the Poor People's Campaign. *The guy seems more interested in putting food on tables than in the presidential nominee. He has no idea that half of us can't hear a word he's saying.*

"Balkan Sobrine."

"Ummm," Peter murmured. He glanced down at the young woman who'd materialized at his side. She looked like a hundred other women he'd seen at the Art Institute: short, slightly-built, with long, dark hair, parted down the middle. Dressed in what he considered the ungodly uniform of the counter-culture—dangling earrings too big for her face, jeans, a work shirt, and no bra.

They bantered for a few minutes exchanging a kind of laconic sexual energy.

"Love the smell." She took off her sunglasses and looked up at him.

Peter adjusted his opinion of her. Her pupils were almost oblong, like a cat's, and the irises were dark green with flecks of gold. They expanded in the sunlight. Against his will, he felt as if he were being sucked into a kaleidoscopic vortex. He looked away and concentrated on her mouth instead. Lowering his pipe, he teased her bottom lip with it. "Have a puff."

"No thanks." She slowly moved the pipe away, continuing to stare at him.

He thought it might go beyond that. He liked her toughness, her spirit, but it made him feel old and jaded. *I'm probably boring the hell out of her*, he thought, so he tried to make a joke about not having any pot. He hoped she'd think he was hipper than he was. But he clearly knew that dressed in a cream-colored linen jacket was as decidedly, and as purposefully, unhip as you could get.

She reached into her jeans pocket, handed him a joint and drifted back into the crowd. He laughed at her audacity and moved in the direction she'd headed. But it was impossible to pick her out of the blue swell of jeans and work shirts.

He decided to walk over to the Band Shell hoping he'd bump into her there, though he wasn't attached to the idea and was open to meeting someone a little more attractive, taller and blond. He could hear the speeches already in progress as he crossed one of the streets that divides the park into separate grassy sections. Jesus, there must be thousands of people here. Maybe I should just hop a subway and head home. But what the hell? Not in the mood to paint today, anyway. He walked towards the Band Shell.

As the day wore on, he got tired and bored. He was sorry he'd bothered walking this far. But as long as he had, he scanned the crowd. He thought about the Hairy Who—his former students—and smiled, imagining the way they'd turn the pro-testors into grotesques and reproduce them on canvas. The long scraggly hair of the demonstrator in front of me—bright green spirals of Medusa curls. That couple, wheeling their kid in a stroller—caricatures of themselves covered with layers of garish paint.

Preferring Matisse's eye over the Hairy Who, Peter shifted his gaze, flattening the same people, outlining them in black, adding texture and color to the solid blue of their jeans and shirts.

His own paintings, none of which hung in his apartment, were abstract swaths of color, cool to the eye, unless you studied them more closely. Some critics compared him to Rothko. Others to Jasper Johns.

He inched next to a young hippie mother dressed in a faded granny gown. She wore round wire-rimmed glasses, like his, and a crown of flowers in her hair. He watched her sitting calmly on a park bench, nursing her baby. And he felt totally unnerved. But at the same time, he couldn't stop staring at her. She must have felt his gaze because she looked up at him and smiled. He had a sudden urge to sit down next to her and lay his head on her shoulder. Instead, he turned away and walked on just as a shout went up from the crowd around him. He craned his neck to see what was going on and spotted the green-eyed girl leaning against a tree, crying. He hesitated for a moment, then steeled himself and pushed through the crowd, working his way over towards the Band Shell.

"My friend accidentally poked me in the eye with her elbow," she said. His rescue fantasies began to dissipate. Suddenly, he heard a loud cheer. He jumped up. A long-haired kid was scampering up a flag pole. Stupid fucker. What the hell does he think he's doing? Peter was relieved when he saw two demonstration marshals run towards the kid and motion for him to get down. But the kid just kept climbing. He's asking for trouble, Peter thought, nervously. Another demonstrator was running towards the flagpole, swinging a shirt in the air. Even from a distance, Peter could see that the shirt was covered with dark stains.

"Jesus," he said to the girl. "That looks like blood. Dried blood."

The girl jumped up beside him, her eye still tearing. "His badge of courage."

Before the marshals could get the kid down, the police grabbed him and carried him off, kicking and screaming.

"Fucking pigs," the girl yelled.

Pigs or not, Peter thought, it doesn't matter much what anyone thinks at this point. He turned in one direction; then another. Then gasped. They were surrounded by hundreds of Chicago's finest.

"We gotta get out of here," he shouted to the girl. The cops began snarling their way towards them. He grabbed her hand, and they started to run. How the fucking hell did I get myself into this? Demonstrators shoved past him, pushing from every direction.

One of them plunged between him and the girl. They were forced in opposite directions.

Everywhere he turned there were angry police. They're coming at me. Every cop in town must be here. Part of him wanted to shout: Let me out of here, you fucking assholes. I'm an innocent bystander. But another part of him didn't feel all that innocent. Just terrified.

He heard what sounded like a gunshot; then the guy in front of him fell backwards, knocking him to the ground. As Peter scrambled to get up, a girl tripped over him. He tried to help her. Jesus Christ, she's bleeding like hell. "Here, here, give me your hand," he said, reaching over to her. Dazed, she grabbed his hand. They both tried to get up. "Shot? Were you shot?" She shook her head no. "Clubbed?" She closed her eyes and nodded.

"Anne, what the fuck . . ." a guy yelled. He lurched towards the girl, on her feet now, but wobbling from side to side.

"She needs a medic," Peter cried. "Get her out of here."

As the guy tried to maneuver Anne through the crowd, everyone around them started choking. Teargas filled the air. Peter covered his burning eyes. A blur of panic seized him. Billy clubs pounded demonstrators. Bodies swung through the park. And nausea ground away in his stomach.

Fuck the police, the New Left, the old Left, and every fucking radical on both sides, he thought, as he gasped for air. He just wanted to escape the insanity and head home. But some primal urge to protect the girl forced him to plunge back into the crowd. He fought the current of demonstrators pressing in the opposite direction. Then he spotted one of the organizers running towards the street. I'll never find her. He was surprised by his regret. Still, he couldn't leave. I see you, damn you. I'll leave when I'm damn ready, he thought as he eyed the police menacing the protestors. His burning eyes still watered from the teargas. He walked around blinking, trying to stare into every face until he realized that the crowd had thinned out—and so had the police.

Jesus, I've never felt so totally vulnerable. I've obviously lost my mind in all this madness. Pushing through the demonstrators, he maneuvered his way back towards Michigan Avenue, hopped the first bus up Michigan to Rush Street, and staggered into a neon-lit bar.

The first vodka, straight up, calmed him down. By the third, his heart stopped pounding in his ears. Then, like the community of drinkers hiked up on bar stools around him, he turned his attention to the 10-inch black and white TV.

A news flash burst onto the screen, temporarily disrupting the Cleavers. Once again he saw the bilge of uniforms attack the demonstrators.

The cameraman cut to the demonstrators. Peter, now on his fourth vodka, searched for the girl's face, but he wasn't sure he would recognize her. He reached for his jacket and was surprised that it wasn't draped on the back of the barstool. Then he realized that he'd left it on the ground near the Band Shell. What the hell, he thought. He slipped off the stool and headed back downtown.

It was almost dark by the time he approached the park again. A group of demonstrators swept towards him as he stepped off the curb. "Thought you only came for the show," she said.

He blinked, wondering if the alcohol might have impaired his memory. This morning, her hair was straight. Parted down the middle. Now it's dancing around her head. He stepped closer to her. No one else has those eyes.

"Show's not over yet," he said, somehow managing to convey his usual ironic distance. But his mouth went dry with the realization that the last smiles of childhood, extinguished years ago, had morphed into a kind of ironic half-sneer. Without a word, he slipped into place beside her. She took his hand. With his other hand, he reached into his pocket and grabbed a Sensen.

He realized they were in some kind of line. At the head of the line, the black man he'd seen earlier was standing on a cart, pulled by two mules. A dozen or so of his followers marched behind him. Peter and the girl and hundreds of white demonstrators followed.

This is completely ludicrous, Peter decided, now that he was a bit more sober. I found the girl. She's safe. I can say good-by and cut out. I'm done here.

"Listen," he started to say. But the light turned red. They were forced to stop in their tracks while the mule train lumbered on. A police squad planted itself in front of them.

"When the light turns green, I'm gonna head out."

"And miss all the fun?"

"Sorry, but yeah. 'Art's long, life short; judgment difficult, opportunity transient.'"

"Brilliant."

"Goethe."

"Impressive. Though you look a lot more like James Joyce. With your round rimless glasses and little mustache."

"Join me?"

"Sorry—not that impressive. Gotta go. Light's turning green."

But the girl didn't move. Neither did anyone else. The police refused to allow them to cross the street. The demonstrators started yelling: "Fuck you, you fucking pigs. Fucking whores." The cops stood their ground.

Angry demonstrators started hurling debris at the cops. "Shit," Peter said, more to himself than to anyone else. He tried to step backward. There were too many demonstrators behind him and to the side of him.

The cops suddenly broke rank and waded into the crowd, lashing out at everyone in sight. Peter covered his head with his arms and tried to get out of their way.

Shit. Fucking shit. I'm never gonna get out of here in one piece.

Peter and Becky saw an opening and started to run. But the police were everywhere—beating on the demonstrators, hitting them over and over again. All of Peter's senses exploded. He could hear bones cracking. Shoulders. Heads. Arms. In a cacophony of deafening sound. He tried to plug his ears. But he couldn't cover his eyes. Blood everywhere. Like gashes of red paint on human canvases. He could feel it prickling his own face. He could smell it.

A blue-eyed cop, a faint scar bisecting his upper lip, leaped in front of him. He looked at the cop's bared teeth. Heard the cop's snarl coming from some dark place deep inside of him. He's gonna kill me, Peter thought. The cop's billy club came crashing down on his shoulder. Peter tried to raise his hands in surrender. But the cop wanted his blood. He kept swinging at

Peter like an angry batter out to destroy the pitcher on the opposing team.

Cursing. Terrified. Peter slipped down to a crouching position. Becky fell beneath him, her forehead streaked with blood. He was so scared, his breath was coming out in short gasps. The stench of blood was making him sick. He scooped her up in his arms, losing his glasses in the crush as they fell to the ground. Then he ferociously pushed through other bleeding demonstrators. Half-wondering if the blue-eyed cop was going to pursue them.

There was no place to hide. Peter moved in a daze. A disembodied club whipped the air around his head. His heart was pounding so violently, he was sure he'd have a heart attack any minute. He kept moving, afraid he'd be beaten to a bloody mess if he stopped.

He raced into the Hilton Hotel and out a back entrance that emptied onto Wabash Avenue—now filled with screaming people scrambling to get away from the police.

This is fucking hell, he thought. He kept running until he got to State Street. Then he descended the steps of the subway, holding the girl close, his heart racing ahead of him.

After they left Northwestern Hospital, he took Becky home with him. He had no choice. She seemed too fragile to survive on her own. I wish to hell someone would take care of me. Or at least hand me a good strong vodka.

She turned and looked at him as they walked into his building. He stared at her for a long moment; then he took her hand, which felt surprisingly soft, and he helped her up the steep stairs to his apartment.

II

Feeling detached, almost weightless, he pulled a couple of beers out of the refrigerator and scrounged around for something to eat. His stomach was still churning. And he wasn't sure he could keep anything down. Just going through the motions, he told himself, as he stood at the stove waiting for the butter to melt in the pan. I can feel my heart racing. But my brain got hijacked by—by— He struggled to locate the right word.

He felt the girl's stare and tried to reconnect his synapses. He glanced over at her. Her face is ashen. She's shaking. Still scared. Jesus, what if she passes out on me? "Hey, you okay over there?" She nodded, barely moving her head. Not exactly reassuring. "I guess the guys who mobilized today's event should have warned everybody to wear football helmets," he said, trying to sound light-hearted. But his earlier playfulness had disappeared. She didn't even attempt a comeback.

He watched her nervously pick at her food. Her face has some color. Skin's almost luminous. Features, delicate. Hadn't noticed that before. Just a kid—eighteen or nineteen, probably. Sitting there with my shirt on. Swimming in it. What the fuck did I get myself into? He still couldn't quite reconnect his brain and his body. But that didn't stop him from wanting to paint her and screw her—in that order.

Peter could hear the noise of the television under the sound of running water. Okay, so it was an adventure, he told himself. What was I even doing there? He took his time washing the dishes, scraping everything off before loading the dishwasher.

After he finished, he lingered in the kitchen, wiping off the counters a second time. The girl's exotic-looking, he thought. Wild hair. Like a gypsy. She's Jewish, he suddenly realized. He grabbed the bottle of vodka from the freezer and almost roared with pain. Putting his hand on his shoulder, he started to rub it. He poured himself half a glass of vodka. Drank it down. Then poured another glass.

Afraid she'd transformed the room by her presence, he did and didn't want to join the girl watching Walter Cronkite on TV. He worried that long after she'd gone, he'd still be subjected to her frenetic force. He leaned against the sink.

The price for seduction turns out to be a lot more than I bargained for, he thought ironically. Still, he couldn't restrain himself from mentally stripping off her clothes, slowly, piece by piece. When he heard her yell, it startled him. He turned away from his thoughts and walked into the living room.

She was sitting on the floor, cheering at the TV screen. There's something absurdly child-like about her. Her streetwise attitude is just that—an attitude. She looks like a twelve-year-old who's just put away her blanky—dressed up in her big sister's long, dangly earrings and put on her ankh. As if that's all the armor she needs to go out and conquer the world. Peter was amused and touched at the same time.

Protecting his shoulder, he lowered his long, lanky body to the floor beside her. Vulnerability was his downfall.

I can smell the dried blood—and the patchouli oil on her skin. If I put my tongue in her mouth, I'd taste her history. Peter felt his body coming to life. He touched the patches of blood on her chest. Put his hand on her child-like breasts. He wanted to feel her slender body.

In the end, he convinced himself that he'd had too much to drink. And he walked her to the El without having sex.

III

Passing Tom's apartment on the way back from the El, he noticed a light in the living room and Tom's hulking silhouette shifting shapes as the curtains flared in and out of the open window.

By the time he rang the doorbell, Tom and Octavia were about to leave. "Come with us," Tom urged. "We're going to a post-convention party to hash over the events of the day."

"I'm beat."

Octavia studied him for a moment. "Actually, you look more beaten up than beat. There's blood on your jeans. "You okay?"

Peter nodded. "Not my blood."

"Were you at Grant Park today?"

"Yeah, I . . ."

"Hey, man, I got the most incredible interviews . . ."

"Come with us. Everyone was there but me."

Peter resisted for a minute; then decided to tag along, hoping to shake off his lethargy. Besides, it was hard to say no to Octavia.

"Love your art," she'd said the first day they met. "Like to see what you're doing now."

"Yeah, man—you're getting way too old to be the young genius."

"It's never too late to be the enfant terrible."

"My article for tomorrow's 'Sun Times' is gonna knock everybody's socks off."

Everyone was stoned when they got to the party. The hosts have good taste, he noted. Great antiques, not that Danish modern stuff. For Peter, antiques had a certain currency beyond their actual worth. That large Persian carpet looks like the one we had in our living room when I was a kid, he thought. He tried to blink away the image of himself studying the Persian carpet while his parents, in their routine and oh-so-calm way, let him and his sisters know how much they despised each other. Torment was the family jewel that bound us together. Yeah, the diamond had many sides. Most of them flawed. Without meaning to, Peter tensed his jaw.

Lucky for me, they, at least, had good taste. He thought about the antiques his father had relegated to the Salvation Army pile after selling the place in Winnetka and moving downtown to one of the Mies van der Rohe buildings. Believes artists should starve, and anyone with a degree from Yale crazy enough to spend his life mixing oil paints could hardly expect to have luxuries and certainly didn't deserve them. Peter cringed. He'd almost had to grovel to get the creased leather chairs and Tiffany lamps.

He noticed Tom standing across the room. Ash dangling from the end of his joint was about to drop onto the Oriental carpet. I wonder if I missed an opportunity with the girl—Becky—to recapture—what? My youth? My identity? He smiled at the thought, not sure where it had come from.

Maybe the real question—the one that grips my insides—is whether it's worth exposing myself. Rather be unknown than mediocre. Sure as hell don't want anybody charting my search for identity. Don't care if people look into my mind. I have plenty to say. But I don't want them licking their fingers on the pulp of my soul.

Peter slumped down on the couch. I want a drink. What am I doing here on the outskirts of my life? Disconnected from everything around me—the party—the people—the Mamas and Papas singing "California Dreaming" for the tenth time.

People standing next to him were talking about the confrontation in the park. Peter felt sick to his stomach all over again and decided to leave. On his way out the door, he noticed Octavia cradling a woman who'd inhaled a whiff of amyl nitrate and had just slid down the wrong rabbit hole. It reminded him of the Pieta. His insides went limp, just as they had the first time he saw the statue of Mary and Jesus when he was a kid. All the fear and impotence he'd experienced that day rushed to his head. I want to be cradled, too. I want to be rocked. A gray stone, two-story building on Ridge Avenue in Evanston flashed into his mind. A recurring image that haunted the gallery of his imagination. When he was a little boy, every time he and his mother drove down Ridge from Winnetka to the city, she would point to a discreet sign in front of the stone building with "The Cradle" written on it. "That's where you came from, Peter," she'd say. Then she'd smile at him, pucker up her glossy red lips and whisper, "Lucky, lucky you. If it hadn't been for me, you could have grown up an orphan."

Years later, he realized his mother had been teasing him. But by then it was too late. He'd already bought the story.

Chapter Three

Lamentations

Anna hated Tuesdays. She used to hate Mondays. Then she realized she hated Mondays because it was hard to find an empty washing machine at the Laundromat on Howard Street. So she changed her laundry day to Wednesday nights.

Actually, it's not doing the wash that upsets me, she thinks, as she struggles up the stairs with her wicker basket. It's the fact that another week's passed. And where has it gone? I'm stuck in a life that should belong to somebody else. Joe keeps telling me to savor my experiences. Not just to nibble at them. What does he know? Every little thing is an experience to him. He makes a story out of it. Like I care about these people I'll never meet. Like anyone cares. This guy gets into my taxi, and you wouldn't believe what he tells me, he says to me, to his friends, to anyone who'll listen to him. Then he makes a whole balagan out of it, with all the gestures and voices. He said. I said. Like a play. My whole life got misplaced. She unlocks the door to her apartment and shoves the laundry basket inside with her foot.

I don't like Fridays much, either, she decides, as she starts folding the laundry she's dumped onto the double bed. Always the guilt on Fridays. Then comes the stomach problems—every Friday night. And all the time wasted on the toilet. I put out the Shabbos candles and challah to remind them they're Jews. No prayers to celebrate Shabbos. I have to say them in my head. He hates everything about religion. Like God cares what he thinks. I try. What else can I do? Maybe we shouldn't have moved out of Garfield Park. And how many Jews do you think are still there, she asks herself, sarcastically.

She glances at the newspaper on the bed. Wednesday, August 28, 1968. She begins gathering up the towels and sheets. She notices an article about police beating demonstrators in Lincoln Park the night before. The summer's almost over, thank God. The heat. Terrible. Not that happy about Wednesdays any more, either since Joe started driving the 4 p.m. to 11 p.m. shift on Wednesdays.

She looks at her Timex. Oh well, it's 11, almost time to chalk up another day. She puts the last towel in the little linen closet and heads into the bathroom.

Sitting on the toilet, Anna wonders what her life would have been like if she hadn't married Joe and hadn't given birth to an alien 19 years ago. From the first moment, I knew I'd never understand that child. And I never did. Still don't. There she was two hours old, a head full of black hair, green eyes wide open, staring at me like she could see into my soul, the nurses oohing and ahhing about how alert she was. Walking at nine months, running at ten, like she couldn't wait to get away from me.

Other children—they cried when they slept away from home the first time. Not her. Other children hid their little perversions. Not Becky. Sitting in the bathtub, her fingers where they shouldn't be. I move her hand away; she puts it right back. It feels good, she says to me. Anna shakes her head in disgust. If she'd been able to completely access her memory, she would have to admit that watching her daughter explore her body had caused a momentary tingle between her own legs.

It was that tingle that had gotten her into trouble. My mother warned me not to let a boy touch my breasts. "Then you'll want to go all the way," she said every time I got ready for a date. Only she said, "vant," not "want." Anna smiled to herself. Joe was a great kisser. I was afraid the blouse I was wearing—that I'd just ironed—would get wrinkled, and she'd know—my mother would know that I let him unbutton it. She was right, my mother.

"You can do better," she said. "He's a schlepper. He'll never be anything more than a schlepper. No education. No nothing. A taxi driver."

Anna sighed. I was nineteen years old. I didn't care if he was a schlepper. For the first time in years she thought about the way Joe used to make her whole body vibrate. A half-smile escaped and creased the left side of her face.

After we got married, in the beginning, oi, we did it every night. Sometimes twice. She remembered how she'd look at him across the room when they were at a party. All he had to do was run the tip of his tongue over his upper lip, and I'd quiver. We were happy. I was happy when I got pregnant. That's what you were supposed to do. Get married. Get pregnant. Have a baby. Have another one. He loved my big breasts. Big to begin with. Even before I got pregnant. Sick of all the looks I used to get walking down the street. The giggles. The jokes whispered behind my back from the time I was in eighth grade. Used to stick out my tongue at all the dirty boys in high school. They stopped looking so much when my stomach was big, too.

I shouldn't have quit my secretarial job at the insurance company. But that was another unspoken rule. Well, I was busy preparing for the joys of motherhood those last two months and too big to waddle into the office, anyway.

She's Joe's child. Has his black curly hair and green eyes, his slender body, nothing like mine. Hates her hair. Irons it flat, like a table cloth in the morning. When I was young, I was proud of my height and my hair. She laughed to herself. Joe. Always said he loved my luscious red hair and luscious big pair. Well, I've chopped off my hair to keep it from thinning even more. And my famous breasts are sagging. She dwarfed small-boned Becky with her teacup breasts, and that made Anna feel awkward. But when she felt particularly peeved at Becky, she liked to point out that Becky had picked up Joe's thick Chicago accent. She, herself, had been able to lose hers. What does it matter now, she wondered. Who was there to talk to? My mother's gone. My old friends from high school have moved up. Sure, we get together once or twice a year. They flatter me. Say how great I look. How young. How well put together. Who are they kidding? They know that moving up for me has been a struggle.

When the old neighborhood went bad, we left the two-bedroom apartment near Roosevelt Road so we could crowd into a one bedroom on the north side. Now this neighborhood's going, too. Changing, they call it now. Two blocks north, on Juneway Terrace, drugs are openly sold out of apartment buildings gone seedy. People call the neighborhood the jungle. Not because of the plants. Almost no green. Just buildings huddled against each other with less than an inch of space between them.

Well, this was a good neighborhood once. Rich Jews lived here. And why not? Just a few blocks from Lake Michigan in a pocket between Chicago and Evanston. Most of them moved to Skokie before we got here. The runaway Jews in their squat little cement look-alike houses. The ones with more money moved to Evanston. Anna didn't know anyone who'd made it further north into Wilmette or Winnetka. And certainly, no one who had made it—or who would have even dreamed of making it to Kenilworth.

She lived two blocks from the last El stop, where passengers had to transfer at Howard Street for the suburbs. It was the end of the line where she confronted broken glass and old newspapers when she got off the train. Or worse—used needles and condoms. Most of the time she didn't even see them. Or if she did, she just pulled herself together and walked on.

Anna heaved a sigh and flushed the toilet. She washed her hands and checked her watch again. There was time for a schnapps before Joe got home. She knew where Becky was—or at least where she had been, even though Becky hadn't bothered to tell her where she was going. *I'm not stupid; I read the papers; I watch the news. All those dirty kids with their "Fuck the Draft" posters. Let them try living in Russia if they don't like it here.*

Opening the bathroom door, she heard muffled sounds. She hesitated for a moment; then plunged into the living room where Becky lay on the couch. Anna noticed that she was wearing someone else's shirt. A man's shirt. Way too big for her. It was buttoned up to the neck. But there was a gap between her neck and the collar. At second glance, Anna also noticed that it was an expensive shirt. Which meant it didn't belong to Richard. She clicked her tongue.

"You scared me," she said.

"Sorry."

Sorry, Anna thought. *I've waited a long time to hear that word from her.* "Were you with that schwartza Janet?" she asked. She avoided looking at Becky, as if the mere sight of her was enough to roil the acid in her stomach.

"I hate that word."

"Among the many other things you hate."

"We got separated at the demonstration."

Anna glanced at her for a moment. Then her eyes darted away. "What happened to your head—and to your eye?" she asked, a little more gently.

"It's nothing."

"I watch the news."

She could feel Becky staring at her. "You could have called." That wasn't what I meant to say, she thought. But she didn't know how to take it back or smooth it over. She'd meant to ask about the bloodstains all over Becky's jeans. She'd meant to ask about the bandage across her head. She'd meant to ask about her eye. She'd meant to ask if she'd been beaten. If she had gotten stitches. If she was in pain. Instead, a trickle of anger had leaked out and tarnished the conversation.

"I should have called? And said what? That I was getting beaten up?"

"What if we needed to get in touch with you?"

"I guess you'd have a problem."

Anna took a step towards Becky. But she wasn't sure what to do with her hands. One nervously explored the other for a moment; then she put both hands behind her back. "If you want, I could take a look at it—at what's under the bandage on your head."

"A doctor already took care of it."

"The eye looks bad."

"Doesn't feel so great, either."

"Did you get stitches?"

"Yeah. A few."

"It's a bad situation. All around, it's very bad."

"Yeah, you're right about that."

"I'm sorry you got hurt. I know what you believe. But they know what they're doing—the government. We don't have all their information. You think we can just walk away?" One sentence too many, she thought. Why do I push it?

"At this point it's really stupid not to walk away."

"You don't walk away from situations. That's not the way it works."

"What if being in the situation is killing you and everyone around you, and . . ."

"That's maybe the way it looks on the outside," she said, raising her voice. "There are certain rules we have to live by in this world." She was beginning to grow into her argument. It felt good.

"No, you're wrong. You can't live by those rules when they stop making sense."

"And then what? Chaos? Like what happened in Grant Park today."

Becky turned away from her mother and sighed loudly enough for Anna to hear her.

Anna's breath curdled in her mouth. "Why? Why do you always have to be different?"

"You mean different from you."

"From anybody with sense. Look at the way you dress. Like a boy. You look like a boy in those clothes. And the hair. Of course, even those hippie boys wear their hair like yours. Wild, crazy."

"I didn't realize you were a fashion expert."

"I'm not an expert on anything. But I know what I know."

"And what's that, Ma?" Becky turned back and looked at Anna directly.

Anna hesitated for a moment.

"That we need more rules?"

"I didn't say that."

"This isn't just about the clothes I wear or about my hair. This isn't just about breaking rules. We have to break them because the f-ing government's forced us to. Because they're breaking the rules—lying their heads off. Oh, oh, yeah, only eight troops were killed today, down from ten yesterday. Yeah. We're winning the war we never should've started. The clothes send a message about the way we feel—different from you and your rules that don't work any more. Tell me something—do they still work for you? Really?"

Anna was taken aback. She could feel the rage building in her stomach.

"I—we—When are you going to stop driving everyone crazy?"

"I don't know, Ma."

"If I was Richard . . ."

"You're not."

"It's a good thing."

"Why? Because if you were Richard, you'd know what a bad ass I am, and you'd find another girlfriend?"

"That's not what I said."

"You didn't have to say it," Becky said, wearily.

"He's a good boy. A nice boy."

"I'm nice, too, Ma."

"Sometimes," Anna said pointedly. "He phoned here an hour ago."

"I'll call him later."

"I thought he'd be there with you."

"He was on the floor of the convention."

"When you get older, you'll see, you'll understand."

"I do understand. More than you think I do. You're the one who refuses to understand. Wake up, Ma," Becky said softly.

Anna looked at her, trying to decode exactly what she was saying. The rage in her stomach began to slowly melt, but she couldn't quite grasp the feeling that had replaced it.

"Your father will be home pretty soon."

"Ma . . ."

"I'm making tuna. You want a sandwich?"

"Ma . . ."

"I better put up the coffee." Anna walked out of the room into the safety of the kitchen.

Careful not to trip on the spot where the linoleum was loose, she skirted her way to the refrigerator and pulled out the mayonnaise. She'd been saving for months so she could replace the faded, ugly floor covering which had once proudly displayed squares with American eagles. It was the bane of her existence. For years she hadn't been able to coax the linoleum back to life no matter how hard she tried. And the building manager refused to listen to her complaints. What else is new, she thought. That's life.

She opened a drawer, spotlessly clean, and carefully lifted out a silver-plated spoon from the set she'd gotten as a wedding present from her parents. Looking at the spoon made her sad. She thought about her mother again. Early on, she'd learned to protect herself from the tap, tap, tap of her mother's vitriolic blows, none of which had been strong enough to knock her out. But all of which had caused her damage. Sometimes her slightest criticism was enough to send my head spinning, she remembered.

Oi, I loved to sing. When I was seven, I could belt out the words to every song on the radio. And every night, alone in the bathroom, in the magical shower, I could sing about lost love. I couldn't tell the difference between my tears and the water coming down on me. She destroyed it. "Your singing gives me a headache," she said over and over till I stopped.

Anna had occasionally resumed singing in the shower, when she was sure neither Joe nor Becky was at home. But, at this point, not even a hum had escaped from her throat for years.

Still, she realized that she wasn't immune to nostalgia. And what she remembered now wasn't her inability to sing anymore. It was the small hump at the crook of her mother's neck, which she'd wanted to press in until it disappeared.

Anna, too, had developed a hump recently. She'd noticed it quite accidentally when she was looking at the back of her head in the mirror one day. She was still in her forties. But she felt old. She'd felt old for a long time. Even when Becky was little, she'd never been young enough to remember what it was really like to be a child.

"Guess what, Ma?"

Anna splashed hot water over the tuna can; then pried it open. She didn't look at Becky, now standing in the doorway. "You know I don't like games." The flutter of a smile crossed her lips. She doesn't want me to be angry with her. She wants my approval even if she doesn't think she needs it.

"I'm gonna move out, Ma."

Anna laughed softly.

"Janet and I are gonna get a cheap place together; we'll go to school at night and work days."

"I see."

"It's not like that."

"Like what?"

"That."

"I didn't say it was."

"You never say it. You never say what you mean."

"Because I don't understand you."

"I understand you. I understand what you mean even when you don't say it."

"Well, I don't understand why you're moving away from your family."

"So you can put the cot in the closet and entertain in the dining room," Becky said, exasperated.

"You always have a smart answer for everything, don't you?"

Anna flung the mayo into the tuna. She mashed it up, pounding it into an unrecognizable paste.

"I'm sorry, Mom. I'm sorry, but I'm going to do it."

"I think I hear your father coming up the steps."

For a moment, Anna allowed herself the pleasure of anticipation. For a moment, her skin tingled, ready to receive the touch of Joe's fingers in her hair. But the rancid smell of the tuna reminded her that Joe sometimes forgot to shower carefully. She withdrew even before he reached the last step and walked down the hallway to their apartment.

"I'll be moving out in about two weeks."

"Sometimes I wonder if there's something seriously wrong with you," Anna said under her breath, as she piled the tuna onto a slice of rye bread.

"So do I."

"There's nothing wrong with you. You're just spoiled. A nineteen-year-old girl doesn't need her own apartment."

"I'm almost twenty. I need my own room. And I'm not spoiled. I'm terrified."

"Then why are you going?"

"Because."

"Because is not an answer I accept."

"Because. Because people who always follow the rules die. Because you have to leave home in order to slay the dragon."

Anna suddenly felt sick to her stomach. *Every day I wake up promising myself that I won't argue with her. And every day I break that promise. There's something about her that drives me crazy. I built up a resentment that makes it impossible to like my own child. I love her. Sometimes I love her. But I don't really like her.*

At that moment, she realizes that Becky knows it. At that moment, she realizes how much she loves Becky. Not just the idea of Becky, but Becky herself. But in the same moment, she realizes that she's lost her forever.

Chapter Four

Word Assassination

Too busy thinking about the climb ahead, she walks across the meadow without really seeing the profusion of multi-colored wild flowers. At the base of a small mountain, she glances over her shoulder. Then re-ties her hiking boots and begins the trek up to the first level.

By the time she gets there, she's panting. Resting on a rock, she reaches into her backpack and takes out her canteen. She lifts it to her lips and can almost taste the cool water as it sloshes towards her mouth. But as soon as she actually samples it, she spits it out. It's warm, bitter, and undrinkable. She looks down at the meadow. She knows she shouldn't go much farther without water. But she continues upward anyway.

The sun's setting. She shivers as she walks. But the top of the mountain's in sight, so she keeps going. Up and up. Chancing it. Then she has to rest again. Has to eat something. She quickly bites into an apple, sucking out the juice. It satisfies her as she eats. But as soon as she finishes, her mouth is drier than ever. She looks up. Just a little way to go. She leaves her backpack behind, taking only a blanket to stave off the cold that is now working its way through her bones.

Finally, she reaches the top. Triumphantly, she looks down at the meadow. She can see it better from this distance. She can see every flower and every blade of grass. She can hear the wind sadly whispering to the meadow like a lost lover. She wraps the old blanket around her as the wind rushes up the mountain carrying messages hidden deep inside its breath. She reaches for a message and opens it. But the writing's indecipherable.

Suddenly, dozens of messages come at her so fast she can't grab all of them. They begin pelting her with a vengeance. Terrified, she tries batting them away, but they stick to the blanket like a hive of white bees, until the only part of her that hasn't been mummified is her face.

And still, the messages continue flying. They strike her face, her mouth, her eyes, sticking to her hair and to her eyebrows, imprisoning her.

"I can't breathe," she screams silently.

Frantically, freeing her arms from the blanket binding her, Carol sits up in bed. Scared. Anxious. For a moment she feels completely out of whack, as if she's been buried under an avalanche of emotions that haven't quite melted, even though her eyes are open, and she's reentered a more familiar world. Or what should have been a more familiar world. The dream has seeped into her waking state making everything slightly unrecognizable.

She glances at Ray sleeping fitfully beside her. She reaches over and is about to touch his long dark, curly hair. But she withdraws her hand instead and slides out of bed.

Though there's a morning chill in the air, she walks over to the open window and breathes deeply, filling her lungs, holding her breath for as long as she can, and then for a moment longer.

She looks at the clock. 8-28-68. 6:00 A.M. She walks to the closet and retrieves her Yoga mat, about which everybody teases her. "Yoga? As in Yogi Berra?" Then she walks into the living room, leaving her dream behind.

Carol had finally grown accustomed to the smells and sounds of the apartment, so different from the house in which she'd grown up. Free to do whatever she wished, whenever she wished, she curled herself into a Yoga position, her legs tucked into a pretzel in front of her. Her mind tightly focused on her meditation, only half-acknowledging that sometimes her freedom hung on her as awkwardly as last year's clothes, now three sizes too big for her. But she was determined to grow into it.

She'd never lived alone before. Not even at the University of Chicago or at Northwestern law school, where she always had roommates. But as soon as she'd gotten the job at Legal Aid, she searched the apartment ads and rented her tiny place in Chicago's Greek Town, which both terrified and mystified her parents.

"Why Greek Town?" her mother had asked rhetorically, when she'd come back to Shaker Heights for the holidays. "Hyde Park was bad enough. For the life of me, I'll never understand why you chose the University of Chicago over Cornell. You were a double legacy at Cornell for god's sake."

Without waiting for Carol's answer, her father coat-tailed her mother, "One of my clients took me to dinner in that area when I was in Chicago last year. The food was atrocious. The neighborhood's iffy. Too close to downtown. It's like living here near the flats. Or little Italy."

"Who do you even know there?" her sister asked sarcastically.

All that was true. She'd chosen the University of Chicago with "all those ethnic" students, as her mother liked to point out, because it wasn't Cornell. She'd spent her whole life at the

Laurel School for Girls. She wanted to taste the world. But it was also true that her friends didn't like coming to Greek Town. Most of them had stayed in Hyde Park after college, but Hyde Park wasn't any safer than Greek Town these days. And Hyde Park was a whole lot more expensive. Besides, she told herself, it was an adventure. She'd wanted to go to Greece since she'd studied Greek mythology in high school. This was the next best thing. Though she'd been to Europe with her family, Europe to them meant Paris, London and Rome.

And she just loved the feel of Greek Town, the smell of it. Even her apartment reeked of olive oil. She loved the closeness of big families who were always in each other's business, yelling and laughing. Warm. She loved being part of a loud, rowdy world where no one told her to modulate her voice. Or sit still. Or stop asking questions. Her next door neighbors had enfolded her, taking her in as if she were some poor lost waif: a tall, sinewy woman, now that she'd finally worked off the thirty extra pounds that had relegated her to the periphery of dating. She was light-skinned and blond-haired and looked totally out of place among the olive-skinned Greeks. Of course, she needed tending, they told her. People to look after her.

There was Ray, of course. Ray had actually gotten her the job at Legal Aid. They'd met at a gathering to discuss grass roots politics, another thing her family found abhorrent, and he'd made a beeline for her afterward. Ray was happy to come to Greek Town. He was happy to be anywhere with Carol. And she had to admit that the look on his face when she entered a room gave her the courage to nudge boundaries that had always kept her dangling on the outskirts of passion. No one had ever looked at her that way before. It was very seductive being so completely loved. But for some reason, she didn't find it quite fulfilling.

Everyone else in Greek Town loved Ray unconditionally. As she was meditating, she flashed on the way he could walk into a restaurant to cheers. Even before ordering, four or five waiters—and the owner—would stand at their table exchanging jokes and baseball statistics. I love to watch him eat, she thought. Food's his second great passion. Next to politics. She smiled thinking about the times waiters brought them new items the cook had just added to the menu. Or when they threw in a complimentary dessert.

Looking Greek, with his dark skin and dark hair, his compact body only a mere inch taller than Carol's, Ray drank retsina and, without a trace of embarrassment, danced Greek dances with the other men. Wilting white handkerchiefs stretched out between them. A bouzouki player strumming away as if this were the last song he'd ever play. It made Carol a little sad.

Ray was surprised to smell coffee brewing when he woke up. He was more surprised when Carol walked into the bedroom holding out a cup for him. He quickly checked the clock. 8:00 A.M.

Sipping his coffee, he yawned, got out of bed, went to the bathroom and brushed his teeth, something he usually put off until just before leaving for work. He liked to savor the pungent tang of coffee for as long as possible. And it was never the same once his mouth had been sanitized. But he was keenly aware that Carol was standing at the bathroom door watching him. Mornings weren't his best time, but she'd been following him around the bedroom.

He took another swig of coffee, shrugged off his shorts, yanked his T-shirt over his head, took a quick smell check under his arms and concentrated on the swell of Carol's breasts under her T-shirt. Alerted by the musky smell that triggered his fantasies, he put his hand under her shirt and his tongue into her mouth as he backed her onto the bed, congratulating himself for knowing exactly where to touch her.

A few minutes later, he was in the shower, renewed and satisfied.

"Okay, babe, be ready in a minute," he called from the bedroom as he dressed. For a moment he was distressed by the paunch that had seemingly appeared out of nowhere. He'd have to cut out the baklava—or not. "Let's get breakfast out before we head down to Grant Park."

The Athena Café on Halsted had become Ray's favorite morning hangout. It had just opened a little over a month ago, but people were already standing in line to get in. Ray was proud of the fact that he'd discovered it before it became popular and secretly even prouder that the owner, Dionysius, usually slipped him in, even though Ray would protest, saying that he'd wait in line like everyone else. Dionysus would simply laugh, grabbing Ray's hand, yelling, "He's my long lost brother."

There was no answer. "Babe," he called again. Still no answer. He walked into the living room. Carol's Yoga mat sat on the floor, but the room was empty. Out of the corner of his eye, he glimpsed a note sitting on the battered oak dining room table, just large enough for the four mismatched oak chairs surrounding it. "Meet you at Athena." He crumpled up the note and tossed it into the air, missing the waste paper basket and hitting the floor, where he left it. Just like my mother, he thought momentarily. Always on the run.

"Hey, how come you snuck out on me?" Ray asked accusingly, in a mock bearish voice.

Carol knew he was only pretending to be angry. But she also sensed a real anger behind the pretense. *I probably should have waited for him*, she thought. For a moment, she considered telling him the secret that had plagued her for the past few weeks. She wanted to get it over with. But she didn't want to chance his walking out of her life, even if she couldn't, or maybe wouldn't, make a commitment. *He's the wall I lean on. The mirror in which I see the reflection of my ideals. In so many ways, he's my validation.* But still, she couldn't apologize for running out on him.

"I mean—I give the girl a good time, and she ups and leaves me before I can get my pants on."

After finishing his mini-rant, Ray looked at Carol for a moment, not quite sure anymore why he'd been irritated. When she rolled her eyes and hinted at laughter, he sat down at the table across from her and changed the subject.

"So, how many people do you think will show up?"

"Tons."

"Tons?"

"Thousands."

"Even after what happened in Lincoln Park?"

"Because of what happened in Lincoln Park."

"I don't know. I think a lot of people will be too scared to come down."

"It's different during the day. Nothing's gonna happen. Lincoln Park—god, it still doesn't seem real. Like a dream you can't quite remember, even though you know it was important."

"Yeah, I know what you mean."

"You scared?"

"Hell, yeah. But there's nothing—nothing in the world that would keep me away."

Carol smiled at Ray.

"Daley, man. Jesus. Thinks he owns the town and can do whatever he wants to."

"He does. And he can. It's like fucking Germany."

"Maybe we should have brought helmets," Carol said, putting her hands on her head, as if she could already feel the billy clubs they'd somehow managed to escape during the rampage in Lincoln Park the night before.

Once they were inside the little car, in the space they'd occupied together dozens of times, everything seemed, at least temporarily, normal and comfortable again. No other world existed except the world inside the bright yellow VW Bug where the smell of new leather and the precision engineering of German mechanics promised that their little world would be safe and inviolable.

But as they edged toward the Loop, anticipation, excitement, and fear hijacked their comfort. Their static two and three-word sentences punctuated by nervous laughter charged the air.

Fifteen minutes later, Ray pulled into a parking lot two blocks from Grant Park.

As they headed for the corner, he put his arm around Carol and pulled her to his chest. Maybe it was the excitement. Maybe the fear. Maybe it was their shared passion for the political that gave him the impetus to pursue the personal.

"I'm not kidding, you know."

"About what?" she asked, slipping out of the hug.

"Getting married."

Carol tamped down an inner scream and presented a learned calm. "Let's not talk about it now. Okay?"

Flexing his hurt like an unused muscle, he reluctantly agreed, irritating Carol. And making her feel guilty at the same time. Maybe I should have told him at breakfast. Maybe there would never be a good time to tell him, she thought fleetingly. He felt her irritation. It irritated him—more than irritated him, really. But by the time they crossed the street, Ray had swallowed his disappointment. Though Carol's annoyance and her guilt continued to bite her.

Ray stopped to chat with someone he knew. It would be easy, she thought. She could have a nice little life with Ray, a good life. They were so compatible, comfortable with each other. But the truth was that Carol didn't want a nice little life. She wanted her world to be filled with magic and mystery. She wanted to take personal dares, not just political ones. To go into the woods of her imagination and grapple with the angels—and the demons—hiding behind the trees. She wanted to finally leave her childhood of stuffed feelings and unspoken words behind. She'd come to believe that she had to really see, to take in everything, because what she'd ignored in the past had cheated her soul.

Her heart began to race. She felt ill and scared and embarrassed and excited at the same time, remembering how she'd lost her sense of gravity that week that Ray was in New York. Remembering how she'd allowed her body to wail with pain and satisfaction. Remembering how she dreamed about those nights again and again. But Ray lived within prescribed sexual boundaries, more turned on by food or by the antics of Abby Hoffman and Jerry Rubin than by the idea of finding new ways to explore her.

Like Ray, Carol believed in the Anti-war Movement and the Civil Rights movement. And she could bulldoze over anyone who stood in the way of progress. But she was too exhilarated by life to confine her passion to political affairs. "We want freedom. When? Now." The national anthem of the Civil Rights movement repeatedly stomped through her brain. But little splinters of delight, having nothing to do with politics, kept exploding, kept pushing her to explore her internal universe, as well.

We know each other too well, she thought, as she looked over at him. Our patterns are already too established for us to take risks. She imagined them moving through life in mini-steps, like twins who've forgotten they're separate people.

Maybe I'll marry Ray some day—in the distant future—after I've gone to Greece. After I've had a life. When I'm middle-aged. Maybe then I'll want to come home to the comfort of his love. But not now. She suddenly remembered the first part of her dream. I still have mountains to climb.

"Jesus Christ, look at that pimpmobile," Ray said, as he rejoined her and they noted a pink Cadillac with tail fins that hugged the curb in front of them.

Both of them started to laugh, breaking the unspoken, and now barely apparent, tension between them.

"Who the hell would drive a car like that?"

"I would," she said.

"Come on."

"No, I mean it. I would love to own that car. That car is me—on the inside."

He laughed again. It made her angry. She didn't want Ray to admire Abby Hoffman. She wanted him to be Abby Hoffman. She remembered the day he'd come over unexpectedly to help her move into her apartment. They'd worked like mad men. Then they'd both collapsed on the living room floor. Dirty and sweaty, they'd unexpectedly made love for the first time in the late afternoon. It was dark when they woke up. Ray rolled over and announced that he was talking a shower. He walked into her newly painted bathroom singing "Lovely Rita Meter Maid."

Carol kicked her dirty clothes to the corner. While she waited for Ray to get out of the shower, she waltzed around her apartment—her very first solo apartment—turning on the lights, watching the living room, bedroom and kitchen come alive. She could see her image in the windows as she danced around each room. She danced over to the kitchen table and took a piece of leftover bagel from the bag. She was starving. Careful not to drop any crumbs, she danced back into the living room, still chewing.

"Pull down the shades, for God's sake," Ray yelled, startling her. She stopped dancing as he circled the room, yanking at the blinds, making sure each gaping window was covered. As he reached the window opposite her, Carol saw her image disappear.

"Did you walk around your parents' house like this?"

Without answering, Carol shimmered past him, grabbing the towel around his middle and yanking it free.

As they approached Grant Park, Carol shook off the memory. She could hear the rumble of demonstrators already assembled. Today they would make a difference. She would make a difference. Nothing and no one could stop the roar of history. Not even Mayor Daly.

She started running. Ray lagged behind. She turned back, noting his look of concern. "Come on," she yelled, without waiting for him.

He caught up with her at the light. "Slow down. Nothing's going on till noon."

"So?"

His caution made her insides growl; the conversation she hadn't allowed herself to begin earlier now strangled her.

"I need to tell you something," she said. "I know it's a bad time, but . . ."

"My God, look at the crowd. There must be thousands of people here already."

"Ray . . ."

"Look, we've both been working hard. I didn't mean to push you about—you know—about what I said earlier." He laughed, trying to regain his dignity. "Though my biological clock's already at half past two." His laughter was forced. He knew it. He knew that she knew it. It made him feel edgy and abandoned. This wasn't the way it was supposed to be.

"Just hear me out." It was too late to stop. The words pounded in her brain.

Ray focused on the sheer number of people milling around the park. He and Carol began weaving through the crowd towards the Band Shell. Though it was only 10:30, they both needed a destination. He didn't want to listen to whatever Carol had to say.

"Hold it till tonight. We can talk then. Promise."

"I had an affair," she blurted out. "A short one. Two nights to be precise."

He turned to look at her. "Why are you telling me this now?" He was angrier about the timing than about her admission.

"I don't know."

"Hey, Carol, Ray," Becky shouted as she bounded towards them.

Carol simulated a wave at Becky. She was happy for the interruption. But Becky caught the tension between Carol and Ray, snatched up the melancholy in the air, and released them so they could recover their public selves.

They scanned the demonstrators, growing in number.

"But why now? I mean what are we talking about? Expiation for old sins? I'm not stupid. I figured it out right away."

She looked at him, astonished.

"I knew the night we ran into him at the Belden Deli after work. Isn't that the guy you're talking about? Peter what's his name? The uptight artist who thought his cock was made of gold."

Ray said all of this in a lawyerly, almost humorous way, as if he were calmly questioning a witness he was covertly trying to intimidate. Because at the same time, he also had to convince the jury that he was really a great guy.

"You knew?"

They couldn't look at each other and felt compelled to keep moving, as if distance could erase knowledge. They wove in and out of groups of twos and tens that multiplied to twenties and fifties. Ray half-noticed the long-haired, skinny female hippies, dressed in granny gowns or jeans. Carol was vaguely aware of their boyfriends, their own hair flowing down their backs. From behind, it was hard to tell who was male and who was female. One guy was bedecked with flowers, no doubt illegally picked. Carol remembered that she'd borrowed bouquets from a cemetery to put on her little table the first time she invited Ray for dinner.

"Yeah, I knew," Ray said.

Friends from work and from their various political involvements called out to Ray and Carol. They melted into the zeitgeist, trying to convince themselves of the possibility that this day could change the downward tilt of the country and begin to make it whole. But they knew their task was impossible, given the animosity between liberals and hawks that had escalated into verbal tantrums on both sides.

When Carol wasn't angry about it, it made her sad—the whole damn stupid collapse into rhetoric. The belief in the domino effect that had catapulted the country into an un-winnable war. When Ray wasn't sad about it, it made him angry.

Ray was relieved because people were beginning to congregate at the Band Shell, diverting attention away from the nausea that was building in his stomach. The air now crackled with excitement as the number of demonstrators blossomed into legions of warriors ready to do battle with the establishment.

"You blushed when he looked at you. And I knew," he whispered to Carol. "But it didn't take a genius to see that he was out of your league—in every way."

Ray's cutting response shocked her. She felt her bones rattle. And behind her sunglasses, her eyes stung with acrid tears. She was surprised by her reaction. She inhaled sharply and swal-lowed hard, forcing herself to concentrate on David Dellinger, listening to him relate statistic after statistic about the Tet Offensive, about the losses, about what the government had lied about and continued to lie about. Demonstrators cheered Dellinger on, yelling, "Right on, right on." But she was silent. Ray was silent. She felt as if she'd been catapulted back to her childhood—as if she'd lost the voice she'd struggled so hard to find.

Ray surprised himself. He hadn't meant to go that far. Hadn't known how angry he was. The hurt was still stuck in the tunnel that led from his throat to his gut. Only the anger had escaped. If he just kept quiet, he thought, maybe she'd for-get what he'd said.

The mobilization had begun. A buoyant peace fell over the crowd, despite the fact that legions of police lurked in the background. Carol refused to allow Ray's anger to hold her captive. She gathered her forces and turned to Ray, speaking quickly without considering the consequences.

"He wasn't out of my league in bed," she retaliated. "He does have a golden cock. He actually enjoyed pleasing me. He wasn't shy about doing things I'd only read about. And he wasn't over and done with in two minutes flat."

Ray gasped. His whole body went slack. The same body that had satisfied him just a few hours before now betrayed him. No matter what he accomplished in his life or who he loved or how he loved her, he knew he'd never be able to forget what Carol had just said and the way she'd said it.

Then almost simultaneously bricking off the hurt, he felt his eyes narrow and his jaw clamp shut. Disgust—anger—a shot of finely tuned hatred coursed through his body, momentarily freeing him from the pain.

"Guess I should have shucked the law books and read 'Masters and Johnson.'"

They looked away from each other. The skirmish was over. Neither of them had won. Both of them felt empty and betrayed. They stood there in the middle of the park surrounded by demonstrators celebrating their coming together, determined to express their support for the Anti-war Movement and for one another, because their passion for the cause was stronger than their fears. Carol and Ray stood among them, shaking on the inside. From a different kind of fear.

Norman Mailer, Jerry Rubin, Carl Oglesby, Tom Hayden and Rennie Davis gave their speeches. The cheering continued. Carol and Ray avoided eye contact and tried to reclaim their armor. Reeling from the rift, Carol wondered how she could ever look at Ray again. But despite their own private sorrow, they began beating to the rhythm of the crowd. By the time enraged police started attacking the crowd indiscriminately, they'd eaten through the day, trying to forget what couldn't quite be forgotten. Suddenly, a guy listening to a transistor radio, started shouting: "They defeated the peace plank! The fucking Democrats defeated the peace plank!"

Ripples of protest and disgust splintered the air.

"Jesus," Ray yelled. "I don't believe it."

A guy with long hair began climbing a flagpole. He reached up, trying to lower the flag.

"Look!" Carol and a dozen other people yelled, as they pointed at the guy.

Anger tore through the air. "Let's confront the damn delegates," someone shouted. "Ask them what the hell they were thinking—defeating the peace plank."

"Move in small groups to the Loop," Hayden yelled.

Furious, Carol and Ray edged forward with the crowd. They tried to cross Michigan Avenue. But the police stopped them. Frantically, they tried to cross the bridges at Balboa and at Congress. The National Guard stood planted in the ground, aiming .30 caliber machine guns and grenade launchers at them.

Terrified, Carol and Ray grasped hands and sprinted north to the Jackson Street Bridge. It was unguarded. They crossed with thousands of other demonstrators surging onto Michigan Avenue.

Then everything seemed to happen at once. Time got compressed. Chaotic. Carol gasped. A soldier, back from Vietnam, who seemingly came out of nowhere, started beating one of the demonstrators bloody. She screamed at the top of her lungs for the police to stop him. Instead they cheered the soldier on. In retaliation, protestors starting hurling anything they could get their hands on at the police. At the first crack, Carol and Ray looked around anxiously for a way out. They were totally surrounded by infuriated cops. Where to go? Cops were viciously attacking with fists, clubs and knees. Grinding their way through the screaming demonstrators. Coming right at them.

Hands tightly linked, Carol and Ray ran, trying to duck the anger that had boiled over into murderous rage. The cops continued blasting their way into the crowd. The sound of crushed bones competed with shrieks of pain and horror. Carol stepped on a pair of sunglasses. Ray stepped over bleeding bodies other demonstrators were trampling in their panic.

They ran towards the Hilton Hotel, panting. Crying. Unable to see or to breathe. They heard the police right behind them—spraying teargas everywhere. Slugging everyone they could. Suddenly, some cops pushed three demonstrators, running next to Carol and Ray, through the window of the hotel. The sound of breaking glass reverberated, threatening the air with menacing shards. Another cop lunged at Carol. Ray jumped in front of her. The cop, distracted by a bottle flying past him, turned away for a moment. Long enough for them to escape. Trying to protect their heads, they ran inside the Hilton. But they still weren't safe. The police slammed into the hotel. Horrified, Carol and Ray watched them beat the demonstrators lying on the floor—on top of the broken glass.

"Move! Move!" Ray yelled, dragging her away from restaurant.

Too terrified to head back towards Grant Park to retrieve Ray's car, Carol and Ray staggered through the hotel to State Street, then to Wabash, and hopped the first El going south.

Carol sat on the curb in front of her apartment building, tears streaming down her face. She wasn't sure if she was crying because of what had just happened in the park, or if she were crying for her and Ray.

Through her tears, she watched a scruffy kid in a Cubs' baseball cap and well-worn Cubs' jacket walk towards them. Unenthusiastically, he extended a bouquet of flowers in their general direction and was surprised when Ray bought a red rose and handed it to Carol without looking at her. She took it and smiled sadly, thinking about the kid's dirty fingernails, which she'd noticed when he handed Ray his change. She knew Ray had given her the flower because he felt sad and didn't know how to tell her. But in the end, the flower didn't feel like a gesture of love to her. It felt as if he'd bought it to put on her grave.

Everything had suddenly changed. Nothing made sense anymore. The ground beneath her feet had shifted irrevocably. She wasn't the same person who had, just weeks ago, cavalierly sacrificed love for a taste of honey. She could tell Ray that a kind of fever had overtaken her and that she'd been captured by an almost lethal sickness that had left her unable to think clearly. But now the illness had passed.

Maybe it was the time in which they lived, she thought. The easy sex, the drugs, even the Buddhist philosophy of detachment, of being free, of welcoming that freedom in others that seduced me into believing I could be free of obligations, as well. I could tell Ray I hadn't realized until today that love wasn't an obligation. It was a commitment. One I hadn't honored.

But she couldn't undo what she'd done. And, really, she didn't want to. Still, she wished she could take back what she'd said. Right now, in this moment when it was too late, she realized that the safety of Ray's love was more important than another death-defying trip to inner space. She loved him truly, if not completely. But the trust between them had been broken. And she was afraid that a patch here and a bit of tape there wouldn't be enough to mend their tattered relationship.

She looked him in the eye and wept for all the pain she'd caused. And for the pain he'd caused, as well. She wanted to touch his face, hold his hand, throw her arms around him and say: We love each other. We're made of the same substance, you and me.

She remembers reading somewhere that love is as strong as death. That mighty waters can't extinguish love or rivers drown it. But she doesn't think that's true. In her experience, love is too fragile to withstand life. Let alone death.

She knows only now, at this moment, that she's been terrified of real intimacy. She's felt that it was a kind of tyranny, really. A tyranny not of compliment or completion but of a conditioned need for the other. And because she understands that intimacy is so illusive, she knows it can't be sustained for very long. That's the paradox. Intimacy can't exist without transparency. But complete nakedness inflicts too much pain for the other to bear.

And still, she looks at him and is overcome with love. The depth of which she's never felt before. It breaks her heart to cross the line for that one brief, completely tender moment. She wants to tell him that he alone is the truth for her and not just a reflection of herself. She sees it in his eyes, too, for a moment— the surprised recognition. But he turns away, walled in by primal abandonments coughed up now like putrefied blood. And the moment passes.

They sit there silently.

Chapter Five

Lost and Found

Octavia's refinement was second nature. She never simply threw on a pair of jeans and a T-shirt, but neither did she bother studying what she wore. She didn't have to. She was the kind of woman who slept in cotton nightgowns someone else had ironed, in a bed somebody else had made.

Tall and slender, she was striking, with her shoulder-length, white-blonde hair obtained without the help of a bottle. Her hair seemed to contradict her brown, almost black, eyes and thick black eyebrows. People turned to look at her when she walked by. But her long, somewhat uneven, nose prevented her from being a so-called American beauty. She didn't like to stand out in a crowd, a trait she inherited from her mother. Though, of course, she did stand out. Short of dying her hair brown and wearing sacks, there was little she could do about it. Still, she knew how to make people comfortable even when she kept them at bay. Her smile relaxed, but didn't encourage. It was friendly, but not intimate. At twenty-four, she was already mature and had a keen sense of herself. At least, most people thought she did.

All that morning, Octavia had been distracted by thoughts of life and death. Mostly of death. And more than distracted, though she tried to keep her feelings at bay. By noon, she decided to drive to Kenilworth during her lunch break. The gallery was closed between 12 and 2, and she trusted Monica to take care of business until she got back. Not that she expected much business that day. Upper Michigan Avenue seems immune from the Convention hysteria, she thought. But she decided that people who had more on their minds than politics probably wouldn't venture out to look at art.

Once inside her car, for a quick moment, Octavia considered heading downtown instead of going home. She turned on the radio to catch the news. When she heard that the anti-war demonstrators had somehow obtained a permit to meet at the Band Shell at noon, she wished she could join them. But, as always, especially now, seeing her mother took precedent. She pulled out of the parking lot next to her gallery and headed north on Michigan Avenue to the Outer Drive.

As she listened to the newscaster describe the thousands of demonstrators milling around Grant Park, she thought about Tom. He's such a little boy. Partly what I like about him, I guess. Love about him, maybe. Resent sometimes, she thought suddenly. She pushed the thought away. Wonder what he was like when he was in kindergarten.

Tom and his friend Peter had graduated from Country Day six years before her. She hadn't known them when she was at school, but she'd heard about them and seen them on campus. Taller and cuter than the other boys. Most of the girls in my fifth grade class had crushes on them, she remembered. He likes to think he's the grown up in the relationship. But he did get me to read the newspaper from cover to cover.

Being essentially a visual person, Octavia found herself weeping over the photos of horrified Vietnamese orphans, victims of a war no one quite understood or seemed to believe in anymore. And despite her own sorrow, it was hard for her to erase those pictures from her mind. She started thinking about them as she drove. Her father still backed the government, so they avoided the topic. And she avoided bringing Tom to the house because he didn't believe in censorship under any circumstances. I wonder if my father's seen the news today. Wonder if he understands why the protestors are so angry. Or cares to understand. I guess I was oblivious for years, too. Maybe he'll wake up. Like I did. I hate any bad feelings between us. Sometimes things have to be left unsaid.

Rounding the bend into Evanston, beads of perspiration broke out on Octavia's forehead. She tried to remember if there was a gas station on Sheridan Road, didn't think so, and headed toward Clark Street. She pulled in and leaped out of the car, leaving the door open.

Five minutes later she was back in the driver's seat, hair combed, face fresh, mouth smelling of peppermint. The little smudge of mascara under her right eye the only clue that she'd just vomited.

She knew and she didn't want to know. Like Vietnam. She was sometimes able to avoid thinking about it for hours at a time. But the minute she turned on the news, there were all those bodies and all those babies with no one to care for them. Her feelings about the war got confused with her feelings about what was growing inside of her. There were rumors about a doctor in Hyde Park whose office was somewhere near the University of Chicago. Friends of friends said the doctor was willing to fix things. And she'd also heard about a doctor in Skokie. Women who could afford it used to go to Cuba. Probably the real reason we broke off diplomatic relations with them, she thought and laughed softly to herself. Tom's leaving for Saigon in three weeks. I'll have to tell him before he goes.

As she drove down her street parallel to Lake Michigan, Octavia felt uncomfortable. Almost like an outsider. I don't belong here, anymore, she thought. But she wasn't sure exactly why or what that meant. Then she remembered the guy. Lawrence Singer. That friend of Tom's from the "Sun-Times." "Kenilworth's synonymous with no Jews or blacks—unless they're the hired help." I couldn't even respond; he was right. I'd just never given it a second thought.

I grew up here. It was just my house. No big deal. Now, I see a gated estate that looks like a small hotel hidden from the street.

The understated opulence of the controlled jungle of ferns, sculptured trees, and exotic flowers made her queasy again. But as she parked her car in the oval driveway, she thought about her mother's eccentric habit of skimping on food. It somehow made her feel less decadent. Still, despite her meager dinners, everyone loved my mother. No one ever turned down an invitation to our house, even though they knew they'd probably go home hungry.

As she walked towards the front door, Octavia remembered all the houses she'd eaten in where guests had left the table feeling empty, despite the fact that they were completely stuffed. I rarely got up from our dinner table unsatisfied, she thought. Then she struggled to recapture that feeling. But couldn't. She sighed, giving into a profound longing that came from some deep, barely recognizable place inside of her.

The door opened before Octavia put her key in the lock. A uniformed maid she'd known all her life smiled at her. "I heard the car," Millie said, scanning Octavia carefully.

"How you doing, Millie?"

"I'm doing just fine, but you look a little pale to me, my girl. I do believe you been skippin' meals since you moved out of this here house."

"How is she?"

Millie averted her eyes. "You know how she is. She'd rather die than complain."

Octavia saw a look of horror cross Millie's face. She mumbled an apology, but Octavia put her arms around her; then slipped off, walking across the expansive marble-floored foyer. Burdened by a now familiar heaviness, she slowly climbed the spiral staircase to her mother's bedroom.

Most people wouldn't have called Helen beautiful. Even when she was young. Her features were too sharp. Her nose a millimeter too long. But she'd been so compelling that it was impossible to look away from her. On that day, she seemed barely present, a fraction of what she'd been. Almost as small as a child.

The coolness, the aloof inscrutable quality that Octavia often displayed in public, collapsed as she took her mother's hand and brought it to her lips. For a moment, she rested her own hand on her mother's still silky skin before she let it run lightly down the side of her mother's face. I can't bear it, she thought. She turned away from the sick woman and forced herself to visualize her mother as she used to be. She imagined her walking down the long hallway into the sunlit library. Her cache of locked files, she suddenly remembered. Who has the key? "They're your legacy," her mother used to tell her.

Octavia thought about the first time she saw her mother put something into the cabinet. I was seven, maybe eight. I pouted when she wouldn't show me what it was. Used to ask her about the secret files. But haven't thought about them for years. Must be part of the family legend that embarrasses her. Maybe some grandparent who was a white-collar criminal. Some uncle who had three wives. Some ancestor who owned slaves. God, I hope not.

Octavia felt a tug and turned back to her mother.

Helen's eyes fluttered open and rested on her. "Did I sleep away the whole day?" she asked groggily.

"I decided to drive up during my lunch break."

Helen forced a smile. "I guess that means you're more worried about me than I am."

"Is the pain under control?"

"Sometimes." Helen's eyes drifted across the room where her nurse, Delores, sat glued to the TV. Between "The Guiding Light" and "General Hospital," there was a newsbreak. The volume was low, but Helen strained to see what was going on.

Octavia smiled. A news addict to the end, she thought. Then tears welled up. She quickly flicked them away.

"Is today a holiday? Why are all those people in the park?"

"They're demonstrating against the war."

Just then there was a shot of dozens of black-helmeted, black-shirted policemen striding into the park.

Helen grew agitated and began picking at her sheet. "They'll line them up and shoot them."

Octavia ran her hand slowly up and down her mother's arm, trying to calm her.

"They'll gas them. We have to do something!"

"It's okay, Mom."

Helen's confusion fractured Octavia's tenuous composure. She began arranging and rearranging the Jugenstil frames on her mother's dresser that held photos of strangers dressed in elegant clothes. When I was little, I stared at this one for hours—the young woman in a long gown who looks like she just stepped out of a Klimpt painting. "Who are those people in the photos?" she'd asked one day. Helen had laughed. "They're just random pictures that someone inserted into the frames I picked up at a little antique shop in New York."

Helen suddenly cried out in pain. Delores leapt up and headed towards the dresser. She carefully measured out the morphine. Octavia put down the heavy, silver-framed photo and watched the morphine travel up the syringe of the hypodermic needle. Then Delores smiled reassuringly, first at Octavia, then at Helen. "No need to suffer, lovey," she said, as she plunged the needle into Helen's almost fleshless arm before Helen could protest.

A few minutes later, Helen closed her eyes and drifted off. Octavia sank back down onto the bed and held onto her mother's hand trying to soak up her essence and intuit her mother's response to the question she hadn't been able to ask.

Octavia had already backed down the driveway when she saw Millie rush from the house. She slammed her foot on the brake and began to panic until she noticed the grocery bag in Millie's left hand.

"Don't eat while you're driving," Millie warned.

"I'll be back tomorrow. To stay for a while."

"Good girl."

Octavia glanced at her watch. If it's two-thirty in Chicago, what time is it in Vietnam, she wondered. "Time to get out of the country," she said out loud.

As she drove away, sadness seemed to permeate every cell in her body. Octavia started to weep. Something she had rarely allowed herself to do. Even when she was a child. It was almost as if she had unconsciously measured her own hurt against some unknown deeper sorrow and had denied herself the right to exercise her grief. She pulled over to the side of the road. It was hopeless, she thought. All of it. The demonstrators in Grant Park don't have any more power to stop the killing in Vietnam than I have to stop my mother's inevitable march towards death. Except for the twinge in her stomach, she felt empty. She turned and looked back in the direction of her house. Then feeling as if her mother was, in some inexplicable way, trying to lift her up from her sorrow, she stopped crying.

She felt the twinge in her stomach again. And, in that moment, she made her decision.

Tom was all revved up by the time she got to his place. He'd spent the day and most of the evening at Grant Park; she'd seen him on television, interviewing the incongruously white hippie Buddhists chanting Ommm along with Allen Ginsberg. She'd worried about his safety and theirs, as she watched the war that had broken out between the demonstrators and the police. The chaos, the blood, the broken heads filled her with anxiety and with a remorse, she didn't quite understand. But underneath that anxiety lay a kind of personal calm, now that she'd made her decision. She tried to relate to Tom's agitation. But he's grown larger than life. As if he's been inflated by the attention of the world watching him and the demonstrators on TV.

As she lay on his bed, Tom paced the room, stopping only long enough to lean down so he could catch a glimpse of himself in the mirror above his dresser. He ran his fingers through his dark hair that fell in ripples to just below his earlobes. He was a rugged-looking guy with an aquiline nose and thin lips. He said he preferred working in the newspaper business to reading the news on TV, where there wasn't enough action. Octavia once teased him, saying, "You don't want to be a news anchor because you'd have to cut your hair." He hadn't laughed.

"Did you see it; did you fucking see what was going on there?" He didn't wait for her to answer. Ripping off his shirt soaked from perspiration, and using it to wipe the sweat from under his arms, he continued ranting. "It was like the air was filled with menace. Fucking police were venomous; they didn't care who they clubbed. I mean, come on. Mr. and Mrs. Citizen sitting in the coffee shop at the Hilton get whacked along with the demonstrators?"

As always, she was momentarily surprised by the light tenor voice coming from such a large, stocky man. She nodded, then sat up and swung her legs over the side of the bed. "Tom..."

"You know if this hadn't been televised, no one would believe it. I was there. And I still don't believe it. I kind of thought you might show up. I looked for you."

"I went to Kenilworth."

"Probably a good thing you didn't come down. It was hard enough to avoid getting clobbered myself."

"I thought about coming down, but . . ."

"Listen, I'm gonna jump in the shower; then we can head over to Grace and Jordan's place."

"Let's just stay in tonight."

"Nah, I'm too revved up"

She nodded. "I guess we can talk tomorrow."

"Hey, we can talk anytime you want to, O." He swatted her playfully with his shirt. Then he headed for the shower, still talking. "My byline's gonna make the front page."

As they stepped out the front door of Tom's apartment building, Peter arrived lugging his melancholy behind him like an extra limb. Tom and Octavia persuaded him to come along.

When they got to the party, Peter moped his way into an easy chair, and Tom disappeared into the kitchen. On the way, he snagged a joint, and Octavia heard him say that grass gives him the push he needs to get out there and do it. Gives him the strength to draw the line between people who care about changing the world and people who like it the way it is. She ran her hand over her stomach and smiled.

She wasn't smoking grass and had sipped only one glass of white wine, so she was more clear-headed than most of the guests. At one point she found herself taking care of a woman having a bad trip. Despite a kind of grace that now enveloped her, she was spent and wanted to leave. Peter looks like he's had enough of the party, too. But Tom's still pontificating about the events of the day, she thought. It bothered her. And it didn't. That's just Tom, she told herself as she sat down on the couch to wait for him.

Someone walked over to the TV and turned it up so they could catch a news special. She watched helicopters patrolling the Dan Ryan Expressway next to the Amphitheater. Dan Rather, clearly out of breath, stood on the street. He looked shaken.

Rather said Senator Abraham Ribicoff strayed from his prepared speech nominating George McGovern. Cheers went up from the party. A clip of Senator Ribicoff inside the Amphitheater flooded the TV screen: "If George McGovern were president, we wouldn't have these Gestapo tactics in the streets of Chicago," Ribicoff shouted.

More cheering from the party. Octavia thought that "Gestapo" was probably a little extreme. The word made her cringe.

The camera cut to Mayor Daley mouthing some words.

"What the hell's he saying?" Tom yelled to their friend Diane, an interpreter for the deaf who could lip read.

Diane stiffened; her mouth dropped; she screamed. "You are not gonna believe this. He said, 'Fuck you, you Jew, you Jew son-of-a-bitch.'"

Octavia didn't know whether to laugh or cry. She looked at Tom standing across the room and tried to signal him as another clip showed a huge group of people on the street. Can we just leave? I feel—I feel—disconnected. Dizzy. On overload.

Dan Rather continued. "About five hundred anti-war delegates are marching from the Amphitheater to Grant Park to join the protestors."

Tom walked over to Octavia carrying a beer. He put it down on the Queen Anne side table, before slipping his arms around her. Barely noticing his presence, she watched the sweat from the beer bottle drip down onto the table and form a puddle.

"What do you say we get out of here and go back to my place?" he asked, kissing her neck.

Octavia swept the water off the table with the sleeve of her silk blouse and placed the bottle on top of a magazine.

She looked at Tom, clearly stoned and hesitated for a moment. I just want to get into bed and pull the covers over my head. Hide, she thought. But in the next moment, she changed her mind. Maybe I should go with him. Just snuggle up next to his familiar warm body. That somehow repelled her. He's not high from the grass. He's high from the demonstrations. Or from his part in them. I'm just too exhausted to care right now. "I think I'd rather just get my car and go home."

"No way," he said, nuzzling her.

She reached for her car keys as he opened the door.

By the time she returned to Kenilworth, it was after eleven. The same melancholy she'd experienced since childhood caught her off-guard as she swung open the car door. But it was different from the sadness she'd felt earlier in the day. The familiar melancholy, she barely allowed herself to recognize, was almost imperceptible. It was like a prick that would sometimes slowly deflate her even in the middle of laughter.

As she walked to the house, her head down, Octavia was startled by a memory of herself and her best friend Marcia. We're sitting in the middle of the driveway. Both of us hoarding a cache of marbles. Marcia has the best cleary. I want it.

Slowly—methodically, I make my moves until Marcia's forced to put her cleary inside the chalk circle. With one flick, the marble's mine. I grab it and jump up.

Even now, Octavia smiles as she remembers the pure ring of her triumphant laughter.

Then I look at Marcia's face and reluctantly hand her the cleary. What my mother would have expected me to do.

She could see the look of anguish on her mother's face. Frances, the night nurse, was trying to drip morphine into Helen's mouth.

"She won't let me come near her with a needle."

Helen indignantly swatted the plastic dropper away, refusing to allow Frances to hijack her freedom. She seemed to have shriveled up even more in the few hours that Octavia had been gone. Octavia could feel the loss in her own bones, as if she were shredding along with her mother. It felt, to her, as if her mother were preparing to return to the womb.

Octavia's throat constricted as she sat down on the bed next to Helen. She kissed her and spoke her name.

"Mein kend, mein einzig kend," Helen whispered.

Octavia looked at Frances totally bewildered. "I had no idea she spoke German."

"She's been speaking like that off and on all week."

Her father appeared in the doorway. Since her mother's illness, night and day had had little meaning for him. Her father slept at odd hours and paced the house during the night like a vampire looking for something to fill the void.

"I didn't know Mom spoke German."

Octavia got up from the bed, walked over to her father, and kissed his cheek.

"She doesn't."

"But I heard her."

"It wasn't German."

Octavia looked at him, amazed. "Yes, it was."

"I thought it was German, too. When I heard her the first time, I was so shocked I couldn't believe my ears. But it's not German. I speak German—perfectly," the old man said. He straightened his back. Octavia could see he was still proud of his ancestry. She would never admit that her great-great-grandparents had come from Germany unless she was pushed. She didn't know why it embarrassed her. But it did.

"What is it then?"

"Some kind of gibberish that sounds like German. She must have heard German spoken when she was a little girl and stored it up in her mind. Now she's recalling it. But it's all mixed up," he said, dismissing her mother's strange language with a wave of his hand."

"Maybe." Read about cases like that. It's possible, she supposed. "She was mostly coherent this afternoon. But I'm not sure she knows I'm here now." She noted the drink in her father's hand. He looks tired, almost fragile, but he's still a big man, a virile, handsome man. Octavia looked like him, with her broad shoulders and straight white-blond hair. The dark eyes and eyebrows had been inherited from her mother's gene pool.

"She knows. She doesn't always have the energy to respond. And the morphine confuses her."

"Mrs. Valesky left some dinner for you, Mr. Herbert," Mille said, as she drifted into the room.

"I'm not hungry, Millie. Thank you."

Millie glanced over at Octavia.

"Have you been drinking your dinners, Dad?"

Millie shook her head, yes.

"Of course not."

"Go down and eat. I'll join you in a few minutes."

Her father left reluctantly, and Octavia told Frances and Millie to get some sleep; she'd sit with her mother for a while. The nurse left. But Millie collapsed into a chair across the room in front of the television that Frances had turned on earlier. Programs were re-running the news of the day. Octavia, glancing at the TV, shuddered when she saw police once again vindictively attacking protestors.

How can that happen in this country; this isn't Germany, she thought, as she pulled a chair up next to the bed and took her mother's hand. She squeezed it lightly, and her mother squeezed back. She knows I'm here, Octavia realized. She was glad she'd come home. But she wasn't quite sure what to do with the exhaustion that was now in command of her mind and her body. I can do this. I'm strong. But I don't know how to do this. She fought back the tears of fatigue and sadness.

"Wasn't German," her mother whispered. Octavia leaned in so she could hear her better. "Yiddish."

Delighted by her mother's humor, Octavia felt an infusion of giddiness. "Is this why you refused to take your medicine? So you could tease me?"

Helen shifted uncomfortably. Then her face collapsed and her jaw shuttered. Octavia watched, thinking her mother had drifted into a tormented dream. The giddiness drained from her body so quickly, it seemed as if someone had given her an injection of sorrow.

"Your history," her mother said suddenly.

My mother's delirious, she thought. But still, in the spaces between her sorrow, something gnawed at her.

"Not enough money."

What can she possibly mean? She doesn't even sound like herself. The cadence is different. The slight accent under her perfect upper-class tone. Maybe I'm just tired.

Her mother sighed deeply, as if the pain of memory was more real than the physical pain she was suffering.

Octavia glanced down at the clock. Eleven-forty-five. I'm dreaming. I'm going to wake up in a few hours and tell my father what I dreamed. And we'll both smile.

She ran her hand across the starched white duvet and looked around. Everything in the room was white: the sheets, the walls, the drapes, the furniture. Even the floors had been painted a glossy white, the sleek expanse broken only by Persian rugs.

Octavia kissed the top her mother's head now bereft of the thick black hair she'd always pulled back into a French twist. From the time she was a child, she'd studied every inch of her mother. She'd spent hours snuggled up inside her mother's cashmere sweaters, trying to discover the something about her that had always remained elusive.

Could this be what I was been searching for? Could my mother be trying to tell me something I can't quite grasp? Yiddish? How could she possibly know Yiddish? I'm not even sure exactly what it is. Has to do with Jews. Old Jews from another world. Claudia Rubin and Joseph Berg from Country Day—they were Jewish, I think. Lea Miller and Kari Davis—at Smith—certainly didn't know Yiddish. Or if they did, never mentioned it. Maybe my mother had had a Jewish friend. But what did she mean about money? Not enough money? Jews had money. The Jews I know have a lot of money. Her mind raced in a dozen different directions trying to compute the information. She wished she could contact an aunt or an uncle or a cousin somewhere. But there were no relatives on her mother's side of the family. Only Great-Uncle Stephen and Aunt Mercedes. They certainly weren't Jews. And Great-Uncle Stephen was dead now, so she couldn't ask him anything. It's like my mother's life began when she met my father.

Helen suddenly winced in pain as she grasped Octavia's hand.

"Don't talk anymore, Mom."

Octavia closed her eyes. She knew two things at once. That it couldn't be true. And that it was. The details mattered. And didn't matter. Suddenly, the world she'd always known and believed in was collapsing. At the same time, the little emptiness inside of her that she'd barely acknowledged before was slowly filling up with pain and recognition. She wanted to weep for her mother and for herself, for the wall of lost memories her mother had erected which had kept her from understanding a side of her Helen had thought she could bury, but which instead had covered her like a shroud. Maybe I can really climb inside of her now, Octavia thought. But she wasn't sure if she were willing.

"You're a member of the Episcopal Church," she whispered in one last attempt to convince her mother and herself that she was lost in someone else's history.

Her mother moved her head slowly from side to side.

Octavia sank to her knees next to her.

Helen began struggling to catch her breath again. Octavia leaned her head lightly on the chest with both breasts missing.

The breathing stopped. Octavia pressed in closer, terrified that she'd lost her mother just as she'd found her.

Helen began to breathe, the rumble of death rattling through her lungs.

Octavia raised her head and looked at her mother's face. "I love you," she said. She put her lips next to her mother's ear and repeated, "I love you," emphasizing the "you."

For a moment Helen opened her eyes and looked at Octavia. All that Octavia could see were her black eyes, not the shrunken body or the bald head. Just the eyes.

"*Ikh hob dich lib, mein kind,*" Helen whispered.

Chapter Six

Night Sweats and Terrors

The empty street slopes down to meet him. The air crackles with menace. He feels it prickling his body—even before he sees the guy. He starts to run. Fast. He hears breathing behind him. Coming closer and closer. Curling around his neck. Choking him. If the tall man breathes on him, he'll die. A dirty yellow bus appears from out of nowhere. Suddenly, he's inside. Safe. He sits down. His heart thumping so loud he wonders if the woman sitting next to him can hear it. He wants her to hear it. The bus stops. The tall man gets on. He's walking towards Mikey. Wearing the usual black shirt and blank pants. Some kind of cap on his head. The same one he always wears. Impossible to see his face. But Mikey knows who he is. The man's chased him before. Lots of times. No one else on the bus knows. They just sit there, staring straight ahead, minding their own business. Maybe the man will breathe on one of them. Leave me alone, he cries silently.

Mikey pulls the cord. Jumps off the bus. He can see Saint Stephan's Church. If I make it there, I'll be okay. He reaches for the familiar pitted brass door handle. Yanks on it. The church is locked. He pounds and pounds till his knuckles are sore and bleeding. The man with the green measles leaps out of the shadows and arches his claws. Mikey keeps pounding. Sweat leaks from every pore in his skinny body. He swipes his arm across his forehead. The man with the green measles pounces on him. Terrified, Mikey clenches his fists. Why are they so huge? He unleashes his fingers and slides his hands down his body. Too big for an eight-year-old. He breathed on me. Mikey whimpers. I have the green measles. I'm blowing up like a human balloon. I'm gonna explode.

"Mike. Mike. Wake up."

Mike is drowning in a sweat of confusion. Then relief. My mother's trying to get me up for school, he thinks.

"The man with the green measles?" Maureen asks.

Mike can't answer yet. His body still feels too big. He needs to give himself time to grow into it.

"Mike. Open your eyes."

"I'm callin' in sick today."

"No, you're not."

He flashes on the image of his red-faced father kicking his mattress. "Get the fuck out of bed, ya little fairy," his father used to yell when he was a kid. "Ya think cause you got a stomach ache, that's reason enough to stay home from school? Ya think anyone cares if I got a stomachache? No. I get up. Go to work. Do my job."

"Can't do it, Mo."

"Get up, Mike. What kind of example you settin' for the boys? Stayin' home from work, just cause you feel like it."

"It's not just the dream."

"He can't hurt you. He's not real."

"He feels real. What's real, anyway?"

"You're a cop, Mike. Not a philosopher."

Mike opens his eyes slowly and follows Maureen as she pulls his uniform out of the closet and hangs it on the back of the bedroom door. He doesn't want to put it on. Not today.

Maybe not any other day, either. If I hadn't gotten married, I'd have gone to law school. Or been a writer. Oh yeah, the old man would have loved that one. I'm a cop. Your brothers are cops. What the hell's wrong with you? Think you're better than us? Huh?

Maureen smoothes out the crease in his trousers. Who is she, this woman I married when we were nineteen? Who were those three boys he could hear yelling in their bedroom down the hall? He tries to locate his high school girlfriend in the body of the woman he's staring at. This Maureen's puffed out like a doughnut. Her little ass's swollen into two round pillows that waddle under her shapeless cotton nightgown. He thinks about the nylon one with the narrow straps and deep pink flowers that she wore on their wedding night. With some kind of flimsy matching robe. And those little high-heeled satin slippers with the feathers in front. Like she was playing some kind of grownup game. Like we both were. First time on a plane for both of us. Didn't know how much to tip the cab driver. Or the bellboy. Nervous. Excited. Drinking in the anonymity—like I could store it up for use against any future regrets. Swallowing the city. Didn't feel like Chicago. "Look there's the Empire State Building. There's the Flat Iron Building." Walking up and down the crowded, dirty streets, garbage bursting from uncovered cans. Our room dingier than I thought it would be. But it didn't matter.

Maureen's hair was all curly and sparkly. She wanted me to look at her. Want her. And I did. It was like the wedding released her. She'd been all shy. Didn't want to get naked before. Now she was laughing. Pulling off her nightgown. Mike releases a groan of infinite possibilities, memories, and meanings.

Maureen bends down, picks up his shoes, and inspects them like a staff sergeant. Look at her fingers. What happened to the long piano player fingers? I can't even recognize those stubby sausages holding my gun. What am I doing here?

Lived my whole life in Bridgeport. We're all safe here in Mayor Daley's neighborhood. Mike starts to chuckle as he sings Mr. Rogers' song to himself, substituting Mayor Daley's name. "It's a wonderful day in the neighborhood . . ." Wish there'd been a Mr. Rogers in my neighborhood when I was a kid.

All the neat little two-story brick bungalows. Kids playing kick ball on the street in summer. Wonder why the Mayor stayed—in the same little house on South Lowe Avenue. Could've moved to the north side. Safe. Familiar, maybe. Yeah. Oh, yeah. Except that the man with the green measles still haunts Mayor Daley's neighborhood.

That time I came home from catechism. My eyes and nose all red from crying. The old man took one look at me and sneered. "Gotta learn how to defend yourself, Mikey. Your big brothers ain't gonna be around to protect you all your life."

I ran out the door—but I didn't have no place to go. So I stood in front of the house. Angry. Ashamed. I hated him. Hated all of them. "I'll huff and I'll puff and I'll blow your house down," I yelled.

"Breakfast's on the table, Mike. Ya better hurry up."

Mike smells sausages cooking and thinks about Maureen's fingers again.

"I don't want no sausages, Mo," he yells.

"Yes, you do. You got a hard day ahead of you. God knows when you'll get lunch."

What the fuck am I doing, he thinks, as he catches a glimpse of himself in the mirror that hangs over the knotty pine dresser with the oak veneer. Maureen isn't the only one puttin' on the pounds. He pats his stomach. Jesus, I'm gettin' to look like the old man.

He takes a moment to admire the thin scar that runs from under his left nostril through his upper lip. Then he slicks back his short light brown hair. Used to be a blond. He snickers. Not true that they have more fun. Just the opposite. "Hey, ya skinny faggot, I'm gonna ram it up your ass, blondie." Like they knew. The damn sixth grade bullies. Wish I could grow a mustache; make me look older. Regulations. Wish I had hard black eyes like my old man's. Not my mother's soft blue ones.

Mike scratches his crotch as if to reassure himself.

When he walks into the kitchen, the two older boys are tossing a box of cereal back and forth, trying to keep it away from Rory, the young one, who's crying in frustration. The little black and white T.V.'s blaring in the background. Sylvester's chasing Tweetie Bird.

"Christ, Mo," he says, grabbing the Wheaties away from the boys and handing it to Rory. "You're almost ten years old, Conner. Quit teasing him."

"Ohhhh, dad swore," Jamie said.

"I didn't swear."

"You said 'Christ.'"

"It's not swearing except if you have cheese on it," Rory says, defending his father.

"What?"

"Cheese. If you say cheese first."

The older boys look at Rory flabbergasted. They both whirl a finger in circles beside their heads—graphically indicating that he's lost his mind. Mike bursts out laughing. He pats the top of Rory's head.

"Cheezes Christ," Rory says. He looks at Mike for support.

"See what he picks up? Watch your language. You're not on duty, Mike."

"Turn off the TV, Mo."

"The boys are watching."

"The news might come on."

Maureen glances over at Mike and turns off the television.

"When Officer Friendly came to my school, this kid in my class asked him if he was a pig," Jamie announces.

"That's just stupid talk," Maureen says angrily.

Rory starts to giggle. "That would be funny—if Officer Friendly was really a pig."

"Oink. Oink," Conner says, pushing up his nose with his middle finger.

Mike bristles, but he doesn't say anything.

"That's enough," Maureen says. She puts a plate of eggs and sausages in front of Mike.

Mike's stomach curdles. He eats the eggs and sausages, anyway. Don't want to hurt her feelings after she went to all the trouble.

Mike calls good-bye to the boys, now pummeling each other in a game of capture the flag.

"Do what you gotta do, Mike. You know what Mayor Daley said. This is our town. We gotta protect it. Those crazies got no right to come in here like they own the place."

"Maybe they're not all crazies, Mo."

"Yeah. Well. I watched them on the news last night. Looked pretty much like crazies to me. Paint all over their faces. Hippies. Long-haired trouble makers."

"If they'd have left the park on time . . ."

"They don't respect the law, Mike."

"I don't know when I'll be home."

Maureen gives him the usual perfunctory kiss on the cheek.

He walks down the front steps of the house. Jesus, if only I could go back and do it over again. What the hell was I trying to prove, anyway, gettin' married so young? You know fuckin' well what you were trying to prove. Fuck all of them.

The smell of incense wafts through his imagination. I loved to look at her body—the blouse of her school uniform pulled tight against her tits because it was from the year before—before she'd started to develop. Surprised the sisters didn't make her go home and change. I'm walking home from St. Edward's; she's walking towards me—coming from St. Anne's—and it's a fuckin' miracle. She stops walking. Stands right in front of me. "I remember you from Mrs. McAndrews' class. How come you never say hello to me?"

I feel my body respond. I blush. I don't have any words.

"Me and Virginia are having some kids over Saturday night. Wanna come?"

I smile nervously at her unintended double meaning. "Yeah," I say, and she whips out her notebook, tears off a sheet of paper, and writes down her address—as if I don't know it.

It wasn't the sex that tormented him. He loved touching her, kissing her, feeling himself explode inside of her. It was the aftermath that killed him. The better the sex, the faster he had to run to escape the man with the green measles breathing down his neck.

She has no idea who I am. Mike stops walking. Maybe she's sorry she married me. Always looking at Joe when she thinks I'm not paying attention. She wants me to be like him—like them.

"Hey, Mike," she calls from the doorway. "God bless."

Maybe not. Maybe it's okay. Feeling a bit lighter, he opens the door to his car. Then he flashes on his dream and shivers.

Could never run fast enough. Or far enough. Just when I think I'm safe, there he is.

Standing on the sidewalk across from the Hilton, Mike is still feeling out of sorts. He tries to convince himself that he's upset with Mo and the way she's let herself go, but he knows that's not what it is. What'd I expect, anyway? She wasn't gonna stay nineteen forever. And she does a great job with the kids, and all. Gets me going. Sometimes to places I don't wanna be. Like here. He tamps down his sudden anger. Trying to make a man outta me. Like my old man. Just what I need.

"Fucking shineys ruin everything," Moderelli said, interrupting his thoughts. Take over everything. Like to send them back where they belong. Or send them to Nam. Bet they'd love that."

Mike looked over at Moderelli without responding. He was tired of listening to Moderelli's rants. He feels like punching him in the face.

"Like to teargas the hell out of them. Rubin. Hoffman. All of them. Shineys."

"What about Hayden and Dellinger?" Mike asked, trying to conceal a half smirk.

"What about 'em?"

"Don't think they're Jews."

"Yeah, well. They got influenced by the damn Jews. That's the way they are. They're good at that."

"What about the Berrigan brothers? Priests."

"Mick priests. Don't see no Italian priests hangin' out with them fuckin' protestors. Hey, my brother 'Antne's' over there. Across the street. Fucker must have busted fifty heads last night."

Mike was amused by the way Moderelli called his brother Antne, and he always made a point of pronouncing "Antne's" name correctly. "Yeah, I see Anthony over there." In actual fact, he was more disturbed by the mispronunciation than he was amused by it. He remembered the way Father Donley used to call him O'Horigan instead of O'Harrigan. As in "Gimme me the chalice, will ya, O'Horigan?" But he was sure he mispronounced plenty of words himself.

"You really enjoy this? Enjoy being in Grant Park?"

"Enjoy? Maybe not enjoy. Yeah. Maybe enjoy. Doin' my duty. Creeps get in the way. Off them. Country'd go straight to hell if them guys was in charge. Always happens that way. Think they can buy people." Moderelli snorted. "Can't buy their way into those fancy country clubs."

"Yeah. You're right about that. But neither can we."

"Yeah, well, who has the dough, anyways?"

Mike wished he could take off his helmet. His head was starting to spin. Everything felt surreal. I'm standing here on this beautiful day. Lake's across the park. Where I want to be. Washed clean. Feel dirty just listening to Moderelli. Hate it when Mo talks like that, too. Not so crude. But comes down to the same thing. Eh—she wants the best for me—for us. Always has ideas. Wish we could move the kids out of Bridgeport. She wouldn't go. We grew up here, Mikey, she'd say. My whole family's here. Your whole family's here. Yeah, I'd think, that's why we gotta get out of here. What if I wasn't a cop? Weird. What would I be if I wasn't a cop? A writer, maybe. I got a lot of stories to tell. Shit. What kind of job is that? Can just hear the old man. You're gonna be a pansy writer? Just cause you can spell, don't mean you know how to write a book. A fairy tale, maybe. Like the man with green measles. Suddenly, it hit him. Maybe he doesn't have green measles. Keep forgetting. Color blind. Sometimes can't tell the difference between red and green. Or brown. One thing for sure, I am not going to bust anybody's head for nothing. Maybe not bust any heads period. They got a right.

"Move, man. Now."

Moderelli nudged Mike into the street.

"Didn't you hear the sergeant?"

Mike looked at him blankly.

"Get ready to form a barricade across Michigan Avenue. We ain't gonna let the white fuckers through."

Moderelli startled Mike back to reality. The sight of the Poor People's Campaign lumbering north bruised his sensibilities.

Jesus Christ, where the hell did they come from, he wondered. He checked out the mule pulling a cart with an old black guy. Maybe not so old. Hard to tell. The black guy's face was slick with sweat. He noticed the shiny black suit. Minister, he thought. Not a priest. He'd given up religion years ago— though he still went to midnight mass on Christmas Eve. Ostensibly for the boys—and for Mo. But the music still brought tears to his eyes, and he sometimes found himself softly humming "Oh Come All Ye Faithful" when he was driving to work.

Mike tried to figure out how many colored people— blacks—African-Americans—he wasn't sure what they wanted to be called—were following the cart. But they started singing "We Shall Overcome," and he got distracted by the music.

The Poor People's Campaign marched past him, crossing at the green light. A few white stragglers made the light and squeezed in behind them. But the other demonstrators were caught at the red light.

Mike started to sweat. Now what?

"Move," the sergeant commanded. "Now!"

The light turned green again. Mike started to move out of the way.

"Get back in line, ya dummy," Moderelli snapped. "They ain't gettin' through."

Mike moved into position between Moderelli and Costigan. They stood shoulder to shoulder across Michigan Avenue, forming a solid human wall.

Suddenly, something came whizzing past Mike's ear. Before he realized what it was, Costigan yelped in pain. A rock came flying at him—from out of nowhere. Maybe from the demonstrators who were trying to push their way across the street. For a moment, Mike just stood there. Dazed.

"Get the fuckers," Moderelli shouted. He flew into the crowd, swinging his billy club. Costigan was right behind him. Blood was flying everywhere. A demonstrator tried to shove Mike out of the way. But Mike automatically pushed back. Relieved he could ward off the demonstrator with just the weight of his shoulder. Then a piece of concrete clipped him on the side of his head. Furious, he raised his billy club and was about to come down full force on another demonstrator scurrying away from him.

"Hey," the guy yelled. "I'm a doctor. You're supposed to protect us. Not beat the shit out of us."

"Then get the hell out of here and help some sick person who deserves it. Or you're gonna get your ass kicked just like everybody else."

The guy just looked at Mike for a moment. Then very calmly said again, "I'm a doctor, man."

Mike looked down at the guy, at least five inches shorter than he was. He was taken aback by his clipped grey hair and the sad bent of his shoulders. He lowered his arm. His insides were shaking. He just stood there. Perfectly still. Listening to the Poor People's Campaign in the distance, singing, "We shall overcome-ah-um. We shall overcome-ah-um. We shall overcome some day-a-a-a-a. Oh, oh deep in my har-a-art. I do believe. We shall overcome some day."

Chapter Seven

Healer

Miles' depression had been eating its way through his body. It had begun quietly, nibbling away at his toes. Then it had eaten its way into his spleen, conquered his stomach, his head that pounded incessantly, and his throat, which always felt constricted. It had finally attacked his nerve endings, still connected to a far off country he'd never wanted to visit, but now couldn't seem to forget.

They'd drafted him as soon as he'd completed his residency. He'd considered heading for Canada, but the thought of tossing eight years of college and four years of a psychiatry residency down the drain forced him to reconsider his options.

Miles headed toward the locked ward to check on his last patient of the day. Maybe they ought to lock me up, too. And while they're at it, the entire government should be committed: Johnson, McNamara and all the other hawks.

Wish I hadn't promised Tom I'd walk over to Grant Park after work. Miles could feel his insides already beginning to churn.

Walking toward the Hilton, Miles tried to shake off his despair. He barely noticed the hordes of people across from Grant Park. Then suddenly—bedlam. His first thought: the inmates are loose. His second was to protect the guys in uniform. But the guys in uniform were brutalizing civilians.

Kids, with blood flowering from their heads, pushed past him, trying to get into the hotel. "Whoa, whoa," Miles yelled at a cop coming at him. "I'm a doctor."

The cop narrowed his eyes to a squint and glared at him. "Then get the hell out of here and help some sick person."

Miles was so shocked he just stared at the cop. The cop blinked, lowered his eyes, and then moved on. Less aggressively, it seemed.

But a moment later, a coke bottle flew past him and hit another cop on the leg. "Commie Jews." The cop held his billy club like a baseball bat and started swinging at anyone in his path. For the first time since he'd gotten back from Nam, Miles felt something besides despair.

"You're supposed to protect us," he yelled at the cop whose bulk dwarfed him. At the same time, he ran towards a guy whose head was bleeding.

The cop raced after Miles. He raised his billy club, about to pounce on him. Again, Miles screamed, "I'm a doctor!"

The cop came down hard on Miles' side; then lurched on towards another target.

Miles staggered. Must have broken a rib, he thought, cringing in pain. He ducked down to avoid any imaginary choppers as he wove his way over to the bleeding guy. He grabbed the kid's arm; then guided him out of the combat zone.

Miles walked into Emergency with the wounded guy, who couldn't stop shaking. The room was filled with other demonstrators. Bloody heads and broken arms. Dazed, whimpering people sat in chairs crammed against every viable surface.

Miles' side ached. The pain felt good. "I'll take care of you," he said to the wounded guy.

One of the demonstrators leaped forward when a nurse called his name. Miles grabbed his chair. "Be right back."

Miles found the attending sewing up another demonstrator. "Brought a guy in who needs attention."

"Who doesn't?"

"Head wound. Needs a few stitches."

"We're swamped. Find an empty cubicle."

"I usually work on what's inside the head, not outside."

"You went to med school; I'm sure you can manage a few sutures."

Miles located a cubicle and led the wounded guy into it. The guy started acting jumpy. Poor kid's just scared, Miles told himself. He's not suicidal, for God's sake.

Since Nam, he'd avoided working with people who'd attempted suicide. Still, sometimes they sneak up on you, he thought. And I don't want to be that person who shows up. Some people look into their secret mirrors and just can't live with what they see.

Wounded guy's not saying a word. Are no words for terror. Miles began suturing the wounded guy's head. Then attacked by a flood of memories, he began feeling ill. He told his patients that when people stop feeling, they die. With him, it was just the opposite. It happened when he had started to feel.

He stared at the blank white wall, so he could reclaim his equilibrium. But he could almost smell the napalm in the air. He clenched his jaw so tightly the back of his neck ached. I'm in Chicago, he thought as he tried to ground himself. He could feel sweat leaking from every pore.

He continued working hypnotically. But he couldn't quite block out the voices of other wounded men he'd treated—or had tried to treat.

"If you keep doing drugs, it'll kill you." That was the party line. I believed it for a while. Absurd. They came to me for help. Waiting in line for a ten, fifteen-minute appointment. Thirty if they were really bonkers. Bonkers. Good psychiatric term. They'd say they didn't want to go back in country. And I'd tell them I understood. I never sat in a trench in the goddamned rain forest, drenched to my very soul. There was no way I could help those poor bastards except to say, "Smoke the stuff." Do whatever you can to forget, to stop feeling, so you can force yourself to go out and face the enemy, knowing that one way or another he's going to get you. Because if he doesn't blow you away, you'll sure as hell end up blowing yourself away with guilt or sorrow.

There was a rapid movement in his Adam's apple. He could hear the tremor in his voice.

"How do you feel?"

"Like shit."

"I mean specifically."

"A little dizzy."

Miles looked into the boy's eyes. "Doesn't seem like a concussion. I think you'll be okay. Let me help you off the table."

"Thanks, Doc. You saved my life out there. Jesus! What the hell happened? This is a democracy, man; it isn't supposed to be like this."

Miles nodded. I couldn't help them. Hell, I couldn't help anybody. Not even myself. He looked into the wounded boy's eyes and saw the reflection of his own nakedness.

"Take care of yourself." The echo of his hollow words ricocheted back at him. He knew the kid knew it. They also knew there would be no deeper relationship.

If I could tell him, maybe the nightmares would go away. Not ready. The irony of it didn't escape him. Maybe in the end, his confession would free him. But it seemed too hard to cross the gap between knowledge and acknowledgement.

When he reached the door, the wounded boy turned and made a peace sign. The beatific look on his face reminded Miles of O'Conner. If only I hadn't decided to surprise O'Conner. They'd had weekend passes. O'Conner had tried to convince Miles to go into Saigon with him, but Miles had declined.

Late Saturday afternoon, Miles was walking around the base, feeling disconnected, hating the sight of khakis and guns. Sick of war talk and tears, sick of feeling worthless. So he decided to hitch a ride from the base and surprise O'Conner.

Even now, he remembered the way he felt as he entered the lobby of the Palace Hotel. Must have been a fabulous place, he thought, as he climbed the stairs.

Heard voices coming from O'Conner's room. Almost walked away. Why didn't I pay attention to my gut? Door wasn't locked. Thought I should knock. Why didn't I? Just burst in, laughing—"Hey, O'Conner." But even in the jumble of the moment—before I knew—I knew.

It all happened in a second. The look on O'Conner's face. His beatific smile gone. Too late to back out. Felt hot and cold at the same time. The whir of the overhead fan buzzed so loudly in my head, I thought the top of it had been blown off.

Barely remember closing the door. Don't remember walking down the stairs. Must have walked down the stairs. Just remember the dirty hallways and the roaches. Hell—the Vietnamese kid couldn't have been more than thirteen or fourteen.

Never talked about it. Two days later, O'Conner's on a mede-vac that's ambushed. Miles shook his head. He could visualize O'Conner throwing himself on top of Johnson, who clung to O'Conner's dog tags.

He felt a shuddering of sorrow, listening to the wounded boy's footsteps as he walked down the hallway. He wanted to run after him and yell, Go to Canada. Instead, he began ripping off the paper cover from the examining table.

Chapter Eight

The Man with Green Measles

Mike stood perfectly still in the middle of the street. People around him were cursing, screaming, running in every direction. Moderelli—or maybe not Moderelli—maybe his brother Anthony—Anknee—he kept hearing the name in his head—was shoving him. Yelling at him to move. He couldn't move. His feet felt like lead anchors. His arm—the one holding the billy club—had gone numb the minute the guy he was about to club shouted at him, "I'm a doctor." Then the buzzing started in his head. The buzzing of fear and guilt. How many Our Fathers and Hail Marys would it take to erase it from his brain? I'm just like them. He tried to untangle the thoughts weaving in and out of the buzzing. Just like them. Supposed to serve and protect. Not maim people for life.

"For fuck sake, ya Irish clod. It's us or them," Moderelli yelled.

In a half-daze Mike saw Moderelli smash a skinny, longhaired guy, delivering his nose to the left side of his face. Blood gushed out in dark puddles. The skinny guy fell to the ground crying. Mike's mouth went dry. Like that time the black comedian marched down his street towards Mayor Daley's house. The neighbors turned their lawn hoses on him and his buddies. Just stood there in my fucking uniform. Didn't say a thing until my boy came running around the corner of the house dragging our hose behind him.

Mike longed to crawl back into bed and wipe out the despair that immobilized him. Then do what, he asked himself. Dream the same dream? Maybe I should just let him breathe on me. Get it over with. Tired of running. So fucking tired of everything. Feels like my bones are melting down. Like they're wax candles lit by anonymous penitents. They stand around for a few minutes watching the candles burn. Then walk off. Like they aren't leaving any residue behind. That's what I am. Residue. The remains of the scared little boy.

"Put on your gas mask, ya crazy Mick," Moderelli screamed. Mike felt the sting of teargas. His eyes watered. He grabbed his mask and jammed it on his face. A barrage of stones and bottles flew at him. His body lurched forward, refusing to pay attention to his brain. Ready for action.

A tall, lean guy dressed in black came running towards him. Mike recognized the lope. He'd seem him a million times in his dreams. Fight or run? It was between him and the guy now. The shouting and swearing was background noise. The chaos of wounded demonstrators and baton-wielding cops blurred, fusing into the periphery of his nightmare. Splashes of green measles all over the guy's cheeks and nose. Some on his forehead and chin. Like pinpricks. Face him or die. Mike raised his billy club and came down hard on the guy's shoulder. He saw the surprise in the guy's eyes. The fear. He was elated. Out of the corner of his own eye, he saw Moderelli club a girl. Once. Twice. She fell. The guy with green measles bent down to sweep her up. Mike whacked at him again and again. Not even sure if he was beating the object of his fear and anger. Or if he was splitting open someone else's head. Sweat was pouring down from his helmet into his eyes. He couldn't see straight.

"Good for you, Mikey. Dammit. Good for you," Moderelli cheered. "Thought you'd lost it. D'ja see the blood?"

Mike stared at Moderelli for a moment. Then Moderelli ran off to wallop another protestor. Another dozen protestors, maybe. Mike raised his billy club high in the air. He allowed himself a moment of triumph. Then he dropped the billy club to the ground. He waded through the crowd of demonstrators and police engaged in an endless permanent nightmare. Then he continued walking up the middle of Michigan Avenue towards the Art Institute. He passed the museum and kept walking. Not sure where he was going. All he knew was that he was walking away.

Chapter Nine

Fragments

Somebody let out a gut-curdling scream. Everybody started running. "Stay calm. Stay calm," Hayden shouted. No one was listening. As soon as Elizabeth spotted the cops closing in, she panicked. Hayden could get down on his hands and knees and beg her not to freak out. But there was no way she was going to just stand there and let some cop mow her down.

"Brad!" she screamed. "Let's get outta here."

Elizabeth and Brad raced towards Michigan Avenue, tripping over their own feet in the rush to exit the park. Halfway there, they realized that for some reason the cops had dropped back. They were safe. One by one the other demonstrators who had run with them, slowed to a halt.

Trying to untangle their panic, Elizabeth and Brad looked at each other. "What the hell just happened?" he asked.

Before she could shrug in response, she heard a nervous giggle. She looked around. "Janet!" she yelled.

Janet sprinted up to them. "Oh man, that was so lame," she said, trying to tamp down her breath.

"What was that about?"

"About a whole fucking lot of tension."

"And what's so funny?" Elizabeth asked.

"You. Me. Brad here. We heard some kind of noise—some popping noise. And Becky screamed. Scared the shit out of me. I covered my eyes—thinking we were gonna get maced again—and accidentally hit her in the eye with my elbow. She screamed again. Then everyone was screaming—running. The pigs started moving in. I ran, too."

They looked back towards the Band Shell where things seemed to have quieted down. At least for the moment.

"Christ, half of Roosevelt's here. Remember that weird girl in Kaplan's class? Kind of pretty, but drugged out half the time?"

"The woman? The one who wore kimonos?"

"Met her on the El coming down. Then ran into her again and dragged her with me when everyone started to run."

Elizabeth looked around as if she expected Sabina to materialize in front of them.

"Said something about an appointment; then disappeared. And by the way, don't you have to get going?"

Elizabeth checked her watch. "I tried calling you yesterday to get the Carter's phone number. Wanted to see if I could pick up the girls tomorrow instead."

"Wasn't home all day. Wouldn't have mattered, anyway. They don't have a phone."

"Guess I should go then, so I can pick them up and head back to Evanston. To relieve Rose. She's been baby-sitting since this morning."

"Relieve Rose or rescue Jenny?" Janet asked under her breath.

"Heard that," Brad said. "I made it to adulthood without too many scars."

"So you say."

"I hate to leave. I feel like I'm abandoning everybody."

117

"I'm gonna boogie outta here pretty soon, too. Let the white folks handle it. You don't mind doing that, do ya, Brad?"

"Hell yeah, I mind. I was counting on you to protect me after Elizabeth leaves."

"Well, rock on, baby. I gotta go find Becky."

As soon as she got into her old Chevy, Elizabeth flipped on the radio. A reporter was interviewing a couple from the suburbs who said they'd come to the park to exhibit their solidarity with the demonstrators. But they weren't exactly sure how to do that. Though it was warm in the car, she shivered, flashing on the day she and Jenny we were crossing Chicago Avenue to join the sit-in at Northwestern. Man nearly mowed us down. Moron, I almost yelled at him—before I noticed the gun and the badge on the seat next to him. Watched his eyes drop slowly to my baby.

So scared the blood stopped circulating in my body. Got mad. So damn mad. Gave his tire a swift kick and walked off without looking back. Still scared every time I see a cop.

Cops lining up around the park when I left. National Guard with guns and bayonets. Should have gone back to get Brad. Probably wouldn't have found him in the mess. Should have tried, she thought as unease embraced her.

She turned off the expressway and headed into a dicey neighborhood. My life's a mosaic. Odd-shaped pieces that don't quite form a whole: mother, wife, anti-war demonstrator, civil rights activist, struggling part-time student. Now I'm about to squeeze in another two pieces. Looking out of the car window, she saw people hurrying off to jobs or making their way to the welfare office, she surmised.

She searched for the street that led to the housing project; then oriented herself toward two high-rise buildings, the Robert Taylor Homes. If I'd brought Jenny, she'd probably be the only light-skinned child within miles. Elizabeth glanced at her face in the rear view mirror. *I obviously had a few white ancestors, too. Like that granddaddy nobody ever talks about. Okay, admit it. You're glad your skin's dark olive. Glad your hair hangs down to your shoulders in waves. Without a relaxer.*

" . . . demonstrator climbing up a flagpole near the Band Shell," she heard on the radio. It shook her out of her reverie.

"What?"

"Crowd's cheering him on."

"You go—whoever you are."

"Wait—wait. Two policemen are running towards the demonstrator. They're pulling him off. They're beating him. The crowd's going wild. I can't see what's going on. Looks like another demonstrator . . ."

She parked the car and just sat there.

"Tide's in; dirt's out."

"A fucking commercial!" Elizabeth turned off the radio and tried to tame her fear and disgust. Finally, she got out and looked around the cracked, gray cement playground next to the parking lot. Not a swing left in tact or a sliding board that hadn't been overturned. Broken bottles littered the ground. *Jesus, how do they live this way?* A heaviness, that wasn't just from the hot, stale air, hung over the place. The only sounds Elizabeth heard were from cars whizzing past on the expressway. *The people in those cars are going someplace, not like the people here,* she thought, as she waited in the deserted lobby for the one elevator that worked. *Wonder what happened to the demonstrator. Brad.* Eruptions of terror spiked her imagination. She wanted to run home to her mother. Only her mother wasn't there.

It was ten minutes before the elevator reached the ground floor. She was about to look for the stairway and climb the fifteen flights to the Carter's apartment when it finally came. Once she got inside, she was sorry she hadn't walked. The sharp smell of urine made her gag. She put her hand over her nose and breathed out of her mouth.

By the time she knocked on the Carter's door, she felt light-headed and dizzy. When it opened, she saw that the whole family had lined up to greet her. Dressed in their Sunday church-going clothes, mother, father, grandparents, and two children seemed waiting either for her command or attack. After she introduced herself, they continued standing at attention, staring at her.

"Is there anything special I should know? Special diets, or anything?" she asked Milene Carter.

"No."

"Ummm, I'll give you my phone number," she stammered. "In case there's a problem—or if you want to check . . ."

"Won't be any problems," Milene said, firmly.

"I meant just in case . . ."

"They know how to act."

"I didn't mean the girls."

"We're all thinkin' about takin' a little trip while Denise and Denetta's with you," Milene said lightly. Her parents nodded their heads in agreement. "Down south."

Elizabeth's heart began to beat wildly. Are they going to abandon the children? Her mouth was dry. Being in their apartment feels like an imposition. I'm taller than any of them. Totally out of place in this neat, clean little place. Surprise, given the chaos and plunder outside. Even the windows shine. Everybody's so neatly dressed. I'm standing here in jeans and a work shirt I've worn for the past three days. Haven't had time to do the laundry. Haven't made a very good impression on them. Should reassure them that Denise and Denetta will be well taken care of, she thought. But the words stuck in her throat. And she wished she were back at Grant Park with Brad and Janet. Any place but here. It was too uncomfortable. And in so many ways, too familiar.

"Here's their suitcases," Milene said. She handed both cases to Elizabeth.

"I guess we'll be going, then."

"You be good girls, now," Milene said.

Elizabeth waited for her to kiss them good-bye. Milene held back. My mother would have been sick with worry, sending me off with a stranger, Elizabeth thought.

The grandparents still hadn't moved. Elizabeth wondered fleetingly if they might be cardboard cutouts.

The little girls hadn't said anything, either. Not hello to her or good-bye to their parents. But they each stuck a thumb into their mouth. She labored to the elevator with their suitcases.

John Carter closed the door to the apartment long before it came.

Both girls jumped into the back seat of the car. Elizabeth shoved a pile of books out of the way, even though Denise and Denetta barely took up half the seat.

She looked into the rear view mirror. Trying to reorient herself, she started singing, "Hey, hey Miss American Pie," as she started the engine. The solemn-faced little girls stared straight ahead.

Why did I get myself into this? Should have told Janet no. Couldn't take in two kids for three weeks, so they'd have a reprieve from the heat and madness of the ghetto. Couldn't refuse. Elizabeth shook her head, remembering how the boiling hot summers would agitate people's nerves. Tapping into fire hydrants for relief doesn't cool off the gangs waging their own private wars against the system, she thought. She knew the projects well—too well. Lived six blocks from here all those horrible years before Mom married J.J. Before we moved to Evanston. That's why she married J.J. Didn't realize it then. Took me years to figure it out. Reason she put up with his rants. Guess she thought anything was better than living in hell. We never looked back. We couldn't.

She eased out of the parking lot. "Took my Chevy to the levee, but the levee was dry."

Denise, the older girl, cracked a smile.

"Like that song?"

"We don't know it," Denise said.

"Don't know it, huh? Well, what song do you know?"

Both girls started to giggle.

She looked in the rear view mirror again and saw them poking each other.

"You tell," Denetta whispered.

"My Mama," Denise said.

"She sing?" Elizabeth asked.

"Noooo," Denetta said, still giggling. "That's silly. That's not what I mean."

"Nobody love me like my mama, and she could be jivin' me, too," Denise sang.

Elizabeth burst out laughing. It eased away some of the tension that gripped her stomach.

"My mama sing that all the time when she workin' round the house. She don't laugh when she sing it, though."

"I don't know that one. What else do you know? Maybe we can sing something together."

"'Sweet Jesus Gonna Ride On.'"

"Oh yeah. I know that one."

"Everybody know that one."

"Well, maybe not everybody."

"We all live in a yellow submarine," Denise started to sing, forgetting about Jesus.

"Now that's a good one," Elizabeth shouted. She sang along with the girls. They started giggling again.

"What's the matter?"

"You sing funny."

"Thought you wouldn't notice."

She needed to find out what was happening in Grant Park. She resisted turning on the radio. She didn't want to break the spell. But her fear started gnawing at her again, as soon as she thought about Brad.

She checked her watch. Hope he heads home before sundown. If there's going to be any violence, it'll be after dark. She half-smiled at the ridiculous and not so ridiculous statement. As if daylight would keep Brad safe. Guess living here taught me to differentiate between "tolerable" brutality and "they're-out-to-kill-every-last-one-of-us brutality. You saw that in person, baby, she said to herself. Saw it from behind locked doors and barred windows. Maybe Brad called the house. Don't remember seeing any phone booths in the park. Michigan Avenue? State Street? Maybe he'll call after I get home—which will no doubt take us forever—hitting the Outer Drive at rush hour.

By the time they reached Evanston, Elizabeth and the girls had almost settled into a kind of friendship. She headed up Sheridan Road past the cemetery and turned left at Dempster, pointing out a couple of little kids running through a sprinkler in front of a huge Victorian house near the lake. "Do you know I have a little girl?"

"Uh huh."

"Her name's Jenny. You're gonna like her."

"Uh huh," Denetta said. She put her thumb into her mouth, pulled herself upright and stared out the window.

Elizabeth turned right on Wesley into a less substantial neighborhood where the houses built in the twenties were much smaller and generally unpretentious. It was hotter and muggier there, away from the lake. But not as hot as it had been on the south side of Chicago. The biggest house on the block was the one next to hers and Brad's. A black family lived there. Elizabeth wasn't sure how many kids they had, because she and Brad had moved in only two months ago.

But she knew the father was a doctor. Before they bought their house, she and Brad had talked to the old, very white woman who lived on the other side of them. The woman had assured Brad that having a Negro family on the block didn't bother her. "He's a doctor, and the family minds their own business," she said, not unkindly. She then turned to Elizabeth and said, pointedly. "You look like a nice girl. I'm sure you'll mind your business, as well."

The old woman also added, by way of explanation: "People who lived in the house before the Negroes were Jews. They broke the covenant and sold to the Negroes."

Elizabeth and Brad returned to their apartment, harried, angry, ashamed, unable to look at each other. It was as if a stranger had blithely paraded their vulnerabilities past them.

"Sure the houses on the block have covenants attached," their lawyer said. "That's why you had such a hard time buying yours, even though you offered them full price." He laughed. "No Jews. No blacks. The sky is falling. They got both in one house."

As soon as Elizabeth opened the front door, she sensed something was different before she realized what it was.

"We're home."

"Sush, you'll wake the baby," her mother-in-law said when Elizabeth walked into the living room. Then Rose looked at the two little girls. Her mouth curled down, as it always did when she disapproved of something. "My God!"

The blood rushed to Elizabeth's head. She wanted to run across the room and slap her skinny, little mother-in-law flaunting her dyed blond hair and flaming red talons. Instead she calmly introduced Denise and Denetta, trying to signal Rose to stop acting as if she'd just met two monsters.

Denetta began tugging at Elizabeth's jeans. "I have to go to the bathroom."

Relieved to move the girls out of her mother-in-law's sight, Elizabeth showed both of them the way, then came back to confront Rose. Her insides still shaking. Rose was one of the few people she knew who could drive her to murderous thoughts. The other person who came to mind at that moment was, of course, her step-father. Elizabeth heard her mother's voice softly admonishing her, "It does no good to shovel up your anger and toss it at others. They just dig it up when they need to and shovel it right back at you. You get enough anger hurled at you, and it eventually buries you. Ask questions. Don't accuse."

"Didn't I tell you I was bringing two children home for a few weeks?" Elizabeth tried to keep the edge out of her voice.

"You told me."

"Then I don't understand. What's the problem?"

"They're so dark."

"Rose!"

"Well, I didn't expect them to be so dark."

"What's the difference how dark they are?"

Rose hesitated, then looked away. "It's just that they're so— so black. I didn't think they'd be so black."

Elizabeth's face stung. She was sure Rose knew that what she'd said was wrong. But Rose couldn't stop herself. And she didn't have any idea how to apologize. "Where's Morrie?"

"Taking the ladder back."

"What?"

"The ladder. He borrowed it from a neighbor."

"What for?

"For the windows."

"The windows?" Elizabeth looked from window to window.

"Somebody had to do it."

Elizabeth's head began to pound. Then suddenly, the pounding exploded. Slowly, she walked over to the toy box that was usually empty because the toys were invariably scattered in every corner of the house. Every toy had been tucked into place. Elizabeth picked them up and tossed them around the room.

"If you don't want to do it yourself, you could hire someone."

"Oh, that's okay. I like it this way." Elizabeth kicked a hand puppet in Rose's direction.

Denise and Denetta came back into the room and stared at the chaos. "Want us to pick them up?" Denetta whispered to Elizabeth.

"No," Elizabeth snapped. Denetta drew back. "I'm sorry, honey. I mean, no thank you," Elizabeth answered more softly. "Maybe you can find something to play with," she said, trying to keep her head from spinning.

"When's Bradley coming home? I brought brisket and roast potatoes."

"He's still downtown."

"In Grant Park?"

"As far as I know." Elizabeth sat down on the floor next to Denetta who was holding Pink Soft Baby. Obviously, Brad hasn't called, she thought. On one hand, she couldn't shake her fear and wished he'd walk through the door. On the other hand, she was glad Brad hadn't come home yet. But she couldn't articulate exactly why. Not even to herself.

Denise was still rummaging through the other toys.

"I don't really understand what you two think you're going to accomplish."

"We think it's important to stand up for what we believe in," Elizabeth said without looking at her mother-in-law.

"Stand up and get knocked down. You're young; you don't know; you'll see. You'll want to get a job; Bradley'll want to get a job in a real law firm—not legal aid—and he won't get it because they'll say you're Commies."

"We're not Communists."

"Looks like it to me."

"Rose, maybe if your people had stood up thirty years ago, they . . ."

"Don't you dare 'your people' me!"

Both children stopped playing and looked up at Rose, standing with her hands on her hips, spewing a wash of anger over Elizabeth.

Elizabeth began slowly beating her chest with her fist, trying to unclog years of unspoken anger and resentment.

"The United States of America is a democracy. This is not Germany," Rose screeched. "Our government is not killing its own citizens for no reason!"

Elizabeth forced herself to speak. "Yes, Rose, they are," she said, quietly. "There was no reason for us to invade Vietnam."

"There were reasons."

"Made up reasons."

"Your hero President Kennedy made up reasons?"

"Yes—not exactly. Maybe he believed them. But he changed his mind. And his brother changed his mind. Bobby knew . . ."

"And some meshugana Arab killed him for it. An Arab. What's he got to do with Vietnam? Did he confuse it with Israel?"

Elizabeth wanted to laugh. Rose had a point. What did Sirhan Sirhan have to do with Vietnam? But she wasn't going to give an inch. "Bobby Kennedy stood up for what he believed in—peace. Regardless of the consequences."

"Nobody wants peace. They only want to protect themselves. We need to protect ourselves. Do you want the whole of Asia to be Communists?"

"I want peace. Brad wants peace. Our friends want peace." I sound like a broken record, she thought.

"Look at the TV. Not what it looks like to me. It's a big mess. People throwing stuff at the police. The police were there to keep the peace. And what did they have to do? They had to knock some people around to protect themselves."

Elizabeth drew in her breath. "Knock people around? You mean in Lincoln Park last night?"

"I mean today. Now."

Elizabeth got up quickly and turned on the TV. "I Love Lucy" spread itself across the screen.

"They interrupted my program. It'll be on the news later."

Elizabeth started to shake. "Mayor Daley gave us permission. It was supposed to be safe."

"Permission or no permission, it doesn't look good to me. You should have told Bradley to come home."

"I think I hear Jenny calling me." Elizabeth turned to Denetta. "I'm going to go in and change her and bring her out here so you can meet her. Okay?"

She needed to calm down, pace out her anxiety, and escape from Rose and from the children, as well.

"I'll get her," Rose said.

"I'll get her."

Black-skinned strangers, Elizabeth thought. The time I overheard her talking to Morrie about me. "Well, at least, the girl isn't so black. And her hair isn't thick and coarse and ugly—you know—like that kinky hair they have."

Rose didn't realize that I heard her. Elizabeth suddenly felt a sharp pain in her stomach. Or maybe she did.

"And don't pick up the toys while I'm gone," she said firmly, as she strode out of the room.

Walking towards Jenny's bedroom, she felt like crying. She thinks I'm crazy. That the only smart thing I've ever done was to marry her son.

Maybe it was.

Elizabeth walked into the room and swept Jenny up from her crib. The little girl nuzzled into her neck.

"Mommy," she cooed.

"Hi, baby," Elizabeth cooed back. She deftly unleashed her soiled cloth diaper, stepped on the foot petal, and deposited it into the already reeking can.

"'Where have all the flowers gone, long time passing?'" she sang. The diaper-changing ritual stabilized her. When her mother had died so suddenly four years ago, she'd unconsciously adopted some of Jennylynn's rituals. She did the ironing every Tuesday while she listened to Studs Terkel on the radio, even though the beds were unmade and dirty laundry spilled out of the laundry basket. She blessed their house every time she entered, thanking God for her family. Even though she didn't really believe in Him, she hedged her bet, unlike her mother who'd been a true believer and had sung out to the Lord every Sunday morning at the AME Church.

After she completed the diapering ritual, she picked Jenny up and held her tightly for a long moment before relinquishing her.

"Let's comb that hair of yours," Rose said, as Jenny tumbled into the living room.

But Jenny noticed Denetta clinging to her favorite doll. She began stomping her foot. "Mine," she cried.

Denetta whirled away from Jenny, pressing Pink Soft Baby tightly to her chest.

"Give the doll back to the baby," Rose said with a false sweetness. "She's only a baby."

Denetta sat down and began singing to the doll.

Elizabeth picked Jenny up in her arms and took her over to where Denetta was sitting. She sat down on the floor in front of her. The two children stared at each other. Each had a thumb in her mouth. But with their free hands, they reached tentatively towards each other's hair. Pink Soft Baby still sat pristinely on Denetta's lap. The two little girls touched each other's hair in awe, rolling it between their fingers, concentrating on the texture, forgetting about everything else, as if they were deep in meditation.

Finally, Denetta handed Pink Soft Baby to Jenny. Jenny hugged the doll, then handed it back to Denetta.

"I hungry," Jenny said.

"Then how about some milk and graham crackers?" Elizabeth put the girls down and walked to the kitchen. The girls scampered after her, leaving Pink Soft Baby on the floor. Rose followed silently.

Elizabeth poured milk into three plastic cups, took out the crackers and set them on Jenny's little table for the three girls.

Brad, she suddenly thought, surprised by her ability to forget her fear even for a moment. She put up the teakettle as Jenny shoved a cracker into her mouth, sprinkling crumbs all over the floor, which her mother-in-law had scrubbed clean.

"You could teach her to use a napkin or a plate," Rose said quietly.

Elizabeth knew she was trying to make it sound more like a suggestion. But she didn't care. "I could. But Jenny might rebel and turn out to be a slob like me."

Rose's jaw clamped shut. Chastised, Elizabeth dropped her eyes. "My mother's house looked like yours," she said, softly. She'd never talked to Rose about her mother before. Perhaps because withholding information about her mother gave Elizabeth a kind of almost opulent power over Rose. But the unexpected memory of her mother's neat, inviting sewing room released a sudden sharp pain in her chest. She wasn't sure she could hold back the tears that were stored just beneath the surface of her daily life.

She looked at Jenny's rust-colored, soft curls, straight nose, and thin lips, like Brad's. How my mother would have loved and cared for my child. How she would have loved and accepted Brad. And his mother. The line between thoughtfulness and thoughtlessness is sometimes permeable. My mother never crossed it.

"I'm sorry, Rose," Elizabeth said. She put her teacup down on the table. "I didn't mean to be sarcastic." Part of her felt like walking over to her mother-in-law and putting her arms around her. That's what her mother would have done. Embrace the enemy. But she knew it would embarrass Rose, because Rose wouldn't know how to respond. Rose is nothing like my mother, Elizabeth thought. She can't help it. I almost feel sorry for the woman with all her hang-ups.

The anger suddenly drained out of her. She felt weak at the knees, as if a familiar, tangible substance had been cut out of her, leaving her freer, but somewhat shaky. She'd come to depend on that anger towards Rose. It buoyed her up when she was down. It propelled her into action. Now she was left with a feeling of lightness.

"All these years I've been your daughter-in-law," Elizabeth said, tentatively. "And it's never quite worked, has it?"

"I don't know what you mean."

"Maybe if we tried to talk to each other, understand each other as two human beings, not as mother-in-law with a capitol "M" and daughter-in-law with a lower case "d," Elizabeth almost pleaded.

"I don't think so."

"I know—I know it's hard for you to accept me, to love me..."

"I accept you."

"I'd like you to love me."

There was a long silence. Rose turned away from her.

"Rose, please look at me," Elizabeth cried. "I don't know who you are. You don't know who I am."

"Maybe it's better that way," Rose said. Then she walked briskly out of the kitchen.

The three little girls were busily sticking their crackers into their cups of milk, giggling, paying no attention to either Elizabeth or Rose.

"It's okay if you can't love me," Elizabeth said to Rose's back. "But maybe you will some day."

Rose didn't answer.

"I will try to love you," Elizabeth called after her.

Rose kept on walking. But it didn't really matter that much anymore. So what if I'm whistling in the dark, Elizabeth thought. It feels better than lying down and allowing waves of anger drown me in sorrow and regret. She leaned back and sighed. She'd come home to her mother, after all.

Chapter Ten

Pulling Strings

Suzanne noticed his black short-sleeved T-shirt with "Make Love Not War" sprawled across the front in iridescent red letters. Noticing her, as well, he angled his way through the crowd towards her. He looked vaguely familiar, but she couldn't place him. Nevertheless, she had an odd premonition and wished he hadn't been able to place her, either.

"Yo, Miz Kaplan," he said before she could escape.

He made her uncomfortable. And not just because she didn't remember his name.

"Yo," she answered, trying to offer a half-smile of appeasement.

He stood directly in front of her. Towering over her. Forcing her to look up at him.

"You don't recognize me, do you?" he asked, accusingly.

"Not really," she admitted.

"Franklin. Lamont Franklin. Tuesday-Thursday, American Lit I. Ten o'clock."

She looked at him blankly for a moment. He continued to scrutinize her. Quickly scanning the room in her mind, she tried to remember the students in her summer school class. Suzanne had great instincts when she conversed with people one-on-one. But she sometimes lacked peripheral vision.

134

"Okay, Lamont Franklin, I give up."

"Yeah, that's what I hoped you'd say."

She caught the insolent swagger in his voice and tried to deflect it by raising her eyebrows, sliding her sunglasses down her nose and peering at him from above the rims. He accepted the challenge and one-upped her, actually leering at Suzanne, encroaching upon her space, and making it hard for her to breathe. She backed into another anti-war protestor, accidentally stepping on his foot.

"Sorry," she said absent-mindedly, as she glanced over her shoulder.

"No problem," the protestor assured her.

But obviously there was a problem. She couldn't exactly pinpoint it. But she didn't want Franklin, Lamont to think that she was nervous. I'm not really nervous, she thought, just glaringly uncomfortable. Maybe because she was a five-foot-two, 28-year-old white woman who looked as if she were still in high school. And he was a black man of indeterminate age looming over her, his biceps bulging, an unmistakable sneer on his face.

"I'm in your class, Miz K."

"Now?"

"Now." He stepped closer to her, forcing her to retreat further. And even though they were in the middle of Grant Park, among a crowd of screaming demonstrators protesting the war, she felt more vulnerable standing in front of Lamont Franklin than she had when a cop had confronted her as she'd walked into the park.

"I am so sorry, but . . ." She stopped mid sentence and stared at him. "Franklin, Lamont. You sat in the last seat. Next to the door. And slammed out as soon as the bell rang."

"Bored," he boasted. "Bored to tears."

"You only came twice."

"Ummm," he said. And she felt caught between his sneer and his invitation. She preferred the sneer and tried to locate her psychological armor. He sabotaged her, gazing at her through sleepy bruised eyes under long curling lashes. Then he smiled at her, a slow, sensual smile, involving his whole body. His red lips parted slightly, exposing his straight white teeth. He might as well have unzipped his pants. His eyes traveled down to her nipples, pressed against her T-shirt, and with a start, she realized that freedom from the confinement of a bra had probably been an idea generated by some guy who was a breast man.

She blushed. What's the matter with me, she wondered. I'm the instructor. He's the student. Just walk away.

"Ummm? As in you're right. I came to class twice."

Wish I'd considered the possibility I might run into some of my students. I'd have worn something a little more appropriate. Not the jeans and the tie-dyed T-shirt. With a peace sign blazoned across the front, no less. The essence of a real authority figure, she thought. She saw herself through Lamont's eyes: a skinny white chick—she hated the word "chick"—with freckles liberally sprinkled across her nose, her dark shaggy hair clipped in a pixie cut. She crossed her arms over her bra-less chest and looked down at the leather sandals one of her former students had made for her. Lent him $200 dollars so he could get started in the sandal business. Nice guy. Black, too. Color has nothing to do with it. Right. Probably wouldn't have loaned the money to a white student. What the hell does this guy want from me, anyway?

"Ummm, as in you gotta pass me."

"And why is that?"

He nodded lazily towards the crowd.

"And?" she asked, mustering up a hint of sarcasm. *How am I gonna get away from him? This is absurd. He's just standing there looking cool. Like he's in control. Like I have to impress him.*

"You're here, aren't you?"

"And?"

"I assume you're not here to line up with the Poor People's Campaign."

"Why would you assume that?" She realized there was an edge in her voice, but at this point, she didn't care. Even though the temperature had dropped a little, it was still August, and August in Chicago was still hot, and her feet were sweating. Even in the sandals. The damp leather gave off a slightly pungent odor that was somehow sensual.

He laughed. "You ain't poor. You ain't black. And I'm not sure yet if you be people."

"Why don't you tell me what you want," she asked, trying to temper her irritation with him—but mostly with herself. She located a route past him and onto one of the paths dividing the park, so she could navigate quickly and lose him as soon as it was feasible. *You know exactly why you're still standing here talking to Lamont Franklin,* she admitted to herself. *You'd have made your excuses to Dick and Jane and been gone five minutes ago. But no one's going to call you a honky bitch.*

"I told you what I want. You need to pass me."

She burst out laughing. "As far as I can remember, you never said a word in class. And you certainly didn't turn in one paper."

"Right on. See, you do remember me."

"And you expect me to pass you?"

"Yeah. I do."

"Because?"

"Because you don't believe in this war any more than I do. Because you don't want to lose one of your students—one of your former students—on the battlefront. Because you're against the draft. And I would be drafted in a hot minute if I weren't in school, which, of course, is why I am in school and why I decided to take your class."

"Okay. I understand why you're in school." She was taken aback by his directness. "But as long as you're there, why don't you do the work?"

"Too busy."

Too busy doing what, she wondered. He adjusted his crotch. She looked down; then flicked away a bead of sweat on her upper lip.

"Yeah, well, there's no way I'm going to pass you."

"Oh, sure there is."

"Why'd you take my class, anyway? There are easier classes."

"Everyone knows your politics."

"So you thought you could take my class, not attend, not do the work and still pass because I'm against the war in Vietnam and wouldn't want to see one of my students drafted?"

He grinned. "Ah, if only you'd spoken so cleverly in class, I'd have stayed."

Her jaw locked shut to imprison the words she wanted to spit at him. At the same time, a wave of uncertainty began nagging at her. Are my classes boring? Derrick—Janet—Becky—Elizabeth—always involved. Sometimes stayed after class and continued talking. Are they trying to protect their grades? Or jack them up?

No, she thought. I can always spot a bullshitter. Lamont Franklin is a bullshitter. That pretty kid Julian from last semester was a bullshitter. Some people think I'm a bullshitter. Think that's how I got my job. Didn't.

The morning she went downtown to Roosevelt University for the interview she scanned her small closet, which held an assortment of jeans and semi-sexy tops bought at the Mexican store. She finally located the one decent outfit she owned at the time. A mustard-colored light wool dress with cap sleeves and a three-quarter length matching plaid coat that she'd gotten on sale at Blums. Never really believed I had a chance. No matter how desperate they were for an instructor.

"You'd have stayed if I'd been cleverer in class, huh? Not so clever of you to say so, Mr. Franklin. Not if you want something from me."

Am I not clever in class? Is clever the test of a good teacher? She remembered her interview with Dr. Andrews, head of the department. A small, pleasant-looking old man with a halo of white hair and pale blue eyes. Asked me a few questions. Seemed remarkably disinterested in my answers. Said he'd get back to me in a few days. Wasn't the least bit nervous during the interview. Given the fact I didn't even have a Masters' Degree, thought it was unlikely anyone would hire me to teach at a university.

"And I do want something from you."

"You'll have to impress me first," she countered. She was determined to stand her ground. But she was beginning to feel maddeningly out of control. Not only did she know what he wanted, she had an almost visceral need to acquiesce. And that scared her. And made her feel queasy. Just like she'd felt that day she went to lunch with her office mate, Joe Flynn. Even now, I feel queasy thinking about it. Asked me why I thought I'd gotten the job. "Guess Dr. Andrews believed me when I said that I was a good teacher."

"Not what I heard," he said, laughing.

139

"What are you talking about? What did you hear?"

"I heard you got the job because you have great legs."

Made my head reel. Thought I'd faint. Didn't feel angry with him for making the comment. Didn't even doubt it. Thought it made sense. Felt hot blood pulsating beneath the skin of my face. Remember looking down at the table, shoving my half-eaten lunch away from me. Wasn't hired because I'm a good teacher or an intelligent woman; was hired because the department chairman dug my legs. And my office mate was telling me this because he was turned on. And he wanted me to know it. And I did. And I didn't. At the time. Lamont Franklin's body is smooth and hairless. And I've never touched a black man. And he knows it. And I can almost feel his breath on my cheek.

I'm standing here, backed up against a tree, confronted by one of my students, probably only a few years younger than I am. And this time the signal's clear. And clearly uncomfortable. If I blink, he'll use it against me. I can feel his lips on my stomach.

"Tell you what," she said, searching for a way to gain control of the situation. "You come to class for the rest of the semester and hand in your back papers, and I'll make sure you pass the course."

"You want me to come to class every day?"

"Yes. Only two classes left."

"Tell you what—that ain't gonna happen," he said, slowly tapping her arm with his knuckles, just below the sleeve of her T-shirt.

His fist felt hot against her skin.

"Well, then," she said. She stopped, not quite sure where to go from there.

"Well, then," he repeated.

"We have a dilemma."

"Not really. I have a pressing need. You have a pressing need." He moved closer to her. "Either you do what you really want to do and make us both happy. Or—you play by the rules and both of us lose." He stroked his upper lip, slowly moving his index finger back and forth.

I cannot allow him to seduce me into giving him a passing grade. "It wouldn't be fair . . ."

"Seduce?" she thought and snickered to herself.

"Fair? Oh now, that's a word that doesn't have any meaning anymore, does it?" He nodded towards the Band Stand where David Dellinger was holding a megaphone to his mouth.

She caught a few words here and there.

"Tet Offensive . . . suddenly, 100,000 new refugees . . . mass graves . . ."

"You know who fights this illegal war as well as I do. Black men, poor white boys, and some honkies with their heads screwed on backwards who get their kicks out of bossing people around."

"Put the blame where it belongs, Lamont."

"I am puttin' the blame where it belongs."

"Maybe the guys who volunteered to go to Vietnam bought the government's lies. Maybe they wouldn't have signed on, if they'd known they were going to be asked to napalm civilians. But you're right."

She was back in familiar territory. In control. "Poor guys don't have a choice; if they don't run, the draft will get them."

"Exactly. Exactly what I'm trying to tell you. You gotta stand up to the man. You gotta stand up to the system. You send me to Nam, and they win again."

"But you have a choice, Lamont. "And so do I."

David Dellinger raised his voice, and they could hear him more clearly.

"We lost 1,000 soldiers in the first two weeks . . ."

"See what I mean?"

"You need to, at the very least, turn in your papers."

"Yeah, well, I could make a lot of promises about doin' that. But you and I both know that ain't gonna happen."

She looked at him for a moment; then she looked away, trying to decide if she'd been outmaneuvered.

When she looked back, he was gone. Lost in the crowd of anti-war demonstrators mobilizing around the Band Shell.

Chapter Eleven

Harvey Bender

Harvey Bender took his emotional temperature at precisely 6:38 every morning. After brushing his teeth, which he flossed after every meal, he gave himself two minutes to decide if he was up or down or merely neutral. On the morning of August 28, 1968, he felt merely neutral. He picked up his electric shaver and studied his reflection in the bathroom mirror as he shaved.

Harvey had a very large head situated on a relatively small body. Though he was five feet, seven—eight if he stretched the truth—a stubborn fear that he was actually a dwarf had persisted since childhood.

Now that he was a lawyer in a big time firm whose name more than hinted at his intelligence, he allowed himself to bypass the size of his head and concentrate on the size of his wallet instead. Most of the time.

Afraid that the electric shaver couldn't quite eliminate his dark beard for an entire day, Harvey anointed his face with shaving cream and began gently sliding a sleek, silver metal Gillette razor over the already smooth surface.

After he finished shaving, he continued staring at himself in the mirror. "Boychik," he said, as he studied the dark circles under his eyes, "you gotta get more sleep."

It wasn't as if Harvey had an active social life, and it wasn't as if he worked such long hours, though he did stay until nine or ten sometimes if he were working on a particularly difficult case with one of the partners whom he wanted to impress. Harvey stayed up late at night listening to classical music. He was educating himself. He listened to Haydn, Mahler, Beethoven, Brahms, and Chopin over and over again until he could identify the composer, the symphony, and the movement. Though, in private, he could admit to himself that he was moved by Tchaikovsky, especially the "1812 Overture," which brought tears to his eyes, he bypassed studying Tchaikovsky's music, as it was frowned upon by serious music lovers.

In order to amaze impressionable young women with his knowledge, when Harvey had a date, he always tuned the car radio to WFMT because they played classical music. And his dates were, indeed, awed, even if they didn't particularly want to date Harvey a second time. One girl he had the hots for, however, had agreed to a second date when he mentioned that he had tickets for the Lyric Opera's production of "Tosca." He had hoped this might ultimately lead to a more intimate relationship, but the girl was busy with her own career and eventually stopped returning his phone calls.

Still, Harvey, a true autodidact, persisted in acquiring knowledge. He bought a membership to the Art Institute and studied the major Impressionists with the same vigor he had lavished on the great composers. If he had not been to the manor born, he would do the next best thing. He would become to the manor adopted. He had his suits tailor made, bought his ties at Sulka, his aftershave at Saks Fifth Avenue. At thirty, he owned an apartment in Hyde Park, near the University of Chicago, one floor below Saul Bellow's, in a neighborhood that had suddenly become chic again. He had studied architectural magazines and had furnished his home entirely himself. Every dish and spoon, every chair and table, every piece of art had been carefully chosen by Harvey. While he couldn't, of course afford the great masters yet, he could afford a few pieces by up-and-coming Chicago artists called the "Hairy Who," graduates of the Art Institute, like Ed Paschke and Jim Nutt, who thumbed their noses at the art establishment. Harvey preferred the Impressionists, of course, which older, wealthier collectors still embraced, but there was something about the ridiculous, unpretentious Imagists that spoke to him.

Harvey had also supervised the reinvigoration of the solid oak floors, the painting of the walls a subtle shade of cream, and the updating of the bathrooms and kitchen so that they maintained the flavor of the late twenties when the apartment building had been built. All and all, Harvey was quite satisfied with his accomplishments, and, though he longed for a woman to fill the empty spaces in his life, deep down he wasn't quite sure he was ready to bring anyone else into his perfect sanctuary. Anyone who might want to change the dishes he'd chosen or re-decorate the dinning room. Sometimes when he could envision that special woman, whose tastes were his tastes, spending the night in his wonderful eighteenth century sleigh bed covered with a thick hand-woven quilt, he had to swallow hard, because he also envisioned her rummaging around in his bathroom or leaving her wine glass on his nightstand.

Harvey straightened his tie and brushed away the imaginary lint on his jacket as he passed the antique, elaborately framed mirror in the hallway situated above the small, antique, mahogany table upon which his cleaning lady neatly stacked his mail.

He glanced down at his highly-polished Florshcim shoes and thought he looked expensive. But part of him wasn't quite sure people would notice. And he wished he could wear the label of his suit jacket on the outside. Winter was great because he could sling his coat casually across a chair with the silk lining and hand-sewn label exposed. And in spring he had his Burberry raincoat, which was also impressive. But in August, it was impossible, unless he could find a good reason to remove his jacket.

Harvey had a long, very successful meeting with a new client, and one of the partners had congratulated him on his brilliance, so he decided to give himself a treat, take a long, very late, lunch break, and cab over to Grant Park from his office on La Salle Street. He was in a great mood, and he wanted to see for himself just what was going on. Harvey did not believe in this war, and he had, in fact, written a cogent letter to the editor of the "Sun-Times" logically and convincingly stating exactly why the United States had been wrong to invade Vietnam in the first place, why the war was an unwinnable quagmire, and why we must now retreat. He didn't, of course, use the word "retreat," though in essence that's what would have to happen.

Three of the partners, self-importance billowing out of flared nostrils in which every visible hair had been clipped, had called Harvey into their individual offices, and without inviting him to sit down on their expensive leather sofas, had let him know that they not only disagreed with his stance but that because he was an associate, he should strongly consider keeping his politics to himself. They had then dismissed him as if he were yesterday's law school graduate.

Luckily, for Harvey, the two founding members of the firm, old lefties who had been raised in the same Workman Circle School as Harvey's father, had not only stood behind him, but had given him permission to use the firm's name in his next letter. Harvey had known, even before he wrote the letter, on which side his bread was buttered. He was canny that way.

Almost as soon as he crossed the street in front of the Hilton Hotel and made his way into the park, he spotted Suzanne Kaplan. She looked disturbed. But who wasn't? After all, that's why they were all assembled here. Though Suzanne had been several years behind him at Northwestern, she'd been in his Modern European Lit class her sophomore year. A large class taught by Don Torcello, the first Italian he'd ever met who had blond hair and blue eyes.

Don was the English Department Casanova. He was also a great teacher, passionate, literate, funny, and dramatic. His classes were filled immediately, and his lectures were well attended. But Harvey was as interested in Torcello himself as he was in "The Magic Mountain" or "Swann's Way." He studied the man, just as he now studied the arts, hoping to learn how to seduce women. All the coeds flocked around Torcello after class hoping he'd notice them. Hoping he'd flirt with them, so they could tell all their girlfriends. Torcello was the essence of cool.

Harvey didn't have either Torcello's Byronic looks or instant charm, but he'd read "The Joy of Sex" and knew exactly how to please a woman. Which he'd done quite well when the opportunity presented itself.

Glad that he had put on his navy blue pin-striped, expensive summer-weight suit that morning in order to impress his new client, Harvey approached Suzanne Kaplan with some trepidation. He had had a major crush on her in college. But she had been out of his league then, and he'd never even spoken to her. And now, here she was right in front of him, still looking like a college student with her freckled nose and short, dark hair, worn in a pixie cut like Audrey Hepburn's.

"Miss Kaplan," he said, his tone of voice perfectly modulated with a touch of irony, a sure sign of sophistication.

"Oh, hi," she said, obviously distracted.

He would have to do something quickly, or she would disappear into the crowd, as she'd continued walking towards the make-shift podium at the Band Shell a hundred feet ahead of them. He began humming the first few bars of Northwestern's Alma Mater.

"Northwestern," she said, without fully engaging.

"Based on Haydn, you know."

"Oh really?"

She turned slightly towards him. Harvey could see by her body language that he had overwhelmed her with his esoteric knowledge.

"I was in your Modern European Lit class."

She cocked her head to the side as if she were studying him, but she continued striding towards the podium.

"It was a big class."

"Torcello."

"Yeah."

"Very suave."

She laughed. "I remember you now. You asked a lot of questions."

"That would be me."

"Howard. Right?"

"Harvey."

"Well, Harvey, what can I say? You obviously asked the right questions. Here you are at an anti-war demonstration, dressed as if you've just had lunch at Jovan and are about to try an important case."

"How did you know?" Harvey asked, delighted.

She laughed again. And though her eyes darted around the crowd, Harvey's perfectly showered body tingled.

"I didn't know, Harvey. But look around. It's the suit. Too expensive for a salesman, not many doctors' offices in this area, but we're not that far from La Salle Street. Nobody else here is dressed like you."

"Very astute powers of observation. I'm an associate at Melvin, Myers, Justice, Courier and Smith."

"You hit the big time."

"Yes, I did."

Harvey wasn't sure if he detected a bit of a smirk, so he decided to take the humble track. Given the fact that she was wearing a god-awful, faded tie-dyed T-shirt with a peace sign blazoned across her chest and blue jeans, he figured she was making her own political statement.

"And what have you been up to since you graduated?"

"Taught at New Trier for a while. Teach at Roosevelt University now. Well, until the end of summer school."

Ah, New Trier, he thought. Excellent. Well, Roosevelt's not Northwestern or the University of Chicago, but it's a university. She can move up from there. "I just wish I could do more about trying to end this war," he said.

"Well, you're here. I guess that says something."

Some people may have found Suzanne's comment and her tone of voice a bit condescending, but completely oblivious, Harvey continued.

"I've been talking to two resisters who burned their draft cards."

"Talking to them, huh?"

"Trying to give them a little advice—pro bono."

Harvey straightened his shoulders and hiked himself up to his full five feet seven or eight inches.

"Good for you."

Harvey was sometimes amazed by his ability to turn on the charm and say just the right thing. Besides that, he was at least a full five inches taller than Suzanne. The guys in his fraternity, one of the two Jewish fraternities on campus, used to tease her about her height. Well, he wasn't one of them, of course. Only the most popular guys dated Suzanne. She'd even gone out with a guy from Sigma Chi.

Word was that she managed to be slightly wild, given the staid times, and Harvey had been surprised to learn that she was intelligent as well. He may have asked most of the questions in their European Lit class, but she knew all the answers in their quiz section, conducted by a grad student intimidated by her brazen disregard for his superior position. Harvey had always gotten a kick out of that, especially as the quiz instructor obviously found Harvey's questions annoying.

"Jesus, look at all the cops," Suzanne said.

Harvey sized up the police, their pants tucked into shiny black boots, their helmets in place, their billy clubs dangling from their belts. Big guys in expensive uniforms, boots, pants, and short-sleeved shirts with their muscles bulging. A whole battalion of Gregor Samsas crawling through the park, almost unnoticed.

"Rennie Davis," Suzanne said, as they approached the Band Shell near the south end of the park. Several men of various ages stood facing the crowd.

Harvey looked up at the short-haired guy, who looked more like him than like the long-haired hippies and wannabe hippies standing next to them. All eyes were focused on Davis. Davis's voice traveled the crowd, exhorting them to protest, on one hand. To keep it in check, on the other. Everyone was amazingly calm, almost languid. As if they realized that their sheer number was enough to send a message. Harvey felt proud to be an American. Proud to live in a country where it was possible to protest the government without fearing that the government would crack down on you and throw you in jail. While he knew that many of the protestors refused to salute the flag and that Abbey Hoffman, aping Kafka, referred to America as Amerika, Harvey felt a stirring in his breast every time he sang "The Star Spangled Banner."

He was sure the demonstrators in Lincoln Park last night had instigated the mess.

"This is a peaceful demonstration. How come so many police are here?" Suzanne asked, looking a little worried.

"Maybe to protect the protestors," Harvey suggested, only half-seriously.

"Oh yeah. That'll be the day."

Suzanne Kaplan's feistiness turned him on. He immediately fantasized walking into the firm's Christmas party with her on his arm. Yes, on his arm. Harvey was just old-fashioned enough to incorporate that into his fantasy. Though on second thought, he might have to amend his fantasy. She was probably the type who would jump out of the car before he could run around and open the door for her.

She would, of course, have to lose the T-shirt and jeans look and the cheap dangly earrings. But by then he would have bought her a pair of cultured pearl earrings to celebrate their fourth month together. The matching necklace would come later. Unlike Harvey, who had struggled to lose his Chicago accent, Suzanne's voice was as accent free as a newscaster's. It was possible that she was from the North Shore, or that she wasn't even a Chicago native. Lots of ex-Northwestern students stayed in the area after graduation. Suzanne Kaplan could pass. If she wore a bra.

"Hey, Janet," Suzanne yelled to a young black woman rushing towards them. Harvey couldn't determine her age, but given the Angela Davis Afro, a look that was fast replacing slick processed hair with a certain demographic, he figured she was probably just past her teens.

"I'm looking for a medic," Janet said.

"You hurt?" Suzanne asked.

"Not me. Becky. I accidentally poked her in the eye with my elbow."

"Ouch."

"She'll live," Janet said, glancing over at Harvey.

Harvey, delighted by the attention, turned his gaze to Janet and was about to introduce himself, hoping that Janet, whoever she was, would mistake him for Suzanne's boyfriend. But Janet dismissed the attempt.

"Me and Becky ran into Staughton Lynd a while ago," she said, as she started to walk away. "Oh, and yeah, I put my paper on your desk."

"Wait a minute, Janet," Suzanne called after her. "You know a guy from class named Franklin?"

"Lamont Franklin?"

"Yes."

"Yeah," Janet said cautiously.

"What's his story in five sentences or less?"

Janet laughed. "Takes a ton of classes and hopes he'll pass enough to keep his deferment. He givin' you a hard time?"

For some reason Harvey couldn't fathom, both women burst out laughing, and Suzanne's face turned crimson.

"Yeah, Ms. K., know what you mean. Peace," Janet said. And within ten seconds, she disappeared, gobbled up by the mostly white crowd of demonstrators.

While Harvey was still in seduction mode, one of the demonstrators began climbing a flagpole nearby. Rennie Davis was still speaking to the admiring crowd, so only a few people noticed at first. Suzanne was one of them. "Oh no," she said, under her breath as she poked Harvey in the ribs.

Two demonstration marshals raced towards the flagpole. But two policemen beat them to it. They started pulling the protestor down. People around them were shouting. Five other policemen quickly joined the first two. They dragged the screaming protestor to the ground and began beating him unmercifully. Harvey was stunned.

"Oh my god," Suzanne shouted.

"Stop. Stop," someone yelled.

"You're gonna kill him."

"Off the fucking pigs."

"What are you doing?"

Hordes of police came wading through the crowd. Confused by the panic surrounding him, Harvey wasn't sure which way to turn. The police were everywhere. Poised to swing at anyone who got out of line. Harvey was as terrified as everyone else. But he knew instinctively that he could maneuver Suzanne out of harm's way if he stayed calm like Rennie Davis. Davis continued standing on the platform, megaphone in hand, an ohm in the midst of impending chaos. But before Harvey could lead Suzanne away, a cop pounced on Davis. Hit him hard on the back of the head. And sent him reeling to the floor of the podium.

For a moment, Harvey couldn't believe what he'd just seen. Then he grabbed Suzanne's arm. "Let's get out of here," he cried urgently. But she stood there, frozen.

"This is horrible. Horrible," she kept repeating.

Someone nearby screamed. A sea of gigantic beetles invaded and began terrorizing anyone in their path. Harvey's sense of identity as a proud American started to shrivel. He felt tears sting his eyes. Everyone around him was crying, as well.

"Teargas," someone yelled.

As if that cry of alarm had finally given her the impetus to move, Suzanne suddenly turned and ran towards the street.

She cut through pockets of dazed demonstrators. Harvey ran after her.

When they got to Michigan Avenue, eyes burning, tears now streaming, they were both panting. Harvey was aware of the sweat rolling down his arms and felt as if he were drowning in salt water and perspiration. The whole experience felt surreal and too real at the same time.

Without speaking, they crossed Michigan Avenue and stood leaning next to the doorway of the Hilton Hotel.

"Jesus," Harvey said. "I can't believe it. What the hell just happened?"

Suzanne was shaking. "It's crazy. The whole thing is insane."

Even with their blurred vision, their eyes were glued to the scene across the street. Both of them felt as if they had somehow escaped from a hell that had materialized from out of nowhere. Other demonstrators, still trying to escape, were running in all directions. The cops were chasing them down. As if they were on a frantic mission.

"We gotta get out of here. Now," Harvey said, without looking away from the park. "But I don't think we can get a cab on Michigan Avenue." He rubbed his eyes, still streaming. "I can't see straight. Maybe we should head over to State Street, grab a cab to Northwestern Hospital."

"Let's just go into the Hilton, find a bathroom, and wash out our eyes," Suzanne said in a monotone, as if her voice were coming from somewhere else.

But they didn't move. They just stood there crying.

"You're a big lawyer," she said, finally coming back to life. "You have to do something about this! Tell people! They'll believe you. Sue the city. We weren't doing anything. We were all innocent bystanders."

"We were protesting."

"So what? Since when has that become illegal?"

"You're right. You're right."

"Let's get out of here."

Suzanne swiped her eyes with her arm. Harvey moved closer to her. For a moment, he worried about his expensive shirt and suit jacket, now totally ruined.

"Maybe we can sue the city."

"We have to do something."

Harvey tried to ignore the bile that coated his throat. Attempting to piece together exactly what had just happened, he suddenly found himself shaking uncontrollably. His illusions had been shattered. Or at the very least, altered.

Suzanne started to cry, clearly not only because of the teargas. "They just came at us—like they hated our guts. My god, it was like they wanted to obliterate every single one of us." She cringed. "To be the object of hatred . . ."

Harvey put his arm around her. "I'll need names of people who were in the park, people who witnessed what went on."

"I can get in touch with some friends who were—who are probably still there," she said, her sobs abating. She allowed herself to lean against him for a moment; then she pulled away. "I have to go back."

"Look," Harvey said, gently. "Given what we just went through, I don't think the police are going to calm down any time soon."

"I know."

"You can't go back to the park."

She hesitated for a moment.

Harvey realized that she was struggling, trying to garner all her resources. He wanted to protect her. Even more than that he wanted to impress her.

"We can't let them win," she said finally. "We can't get into the boxcars again, thinking we can save our asses if we don't protest."

Harvey looked at her for what seemed like a long, long time. Every rational bone in his body screamed, Go. Go back to your office. Go home. Go anywhere but across the street to Grant Park.

Finally, he took her hand. "Let's go."

"I'm not leaving Grant Park," she said, fear obviously lurking behind her bravado.

"I know."

They began walking to the corner.

Somehow, despite his fear and his losses, despite the ordeal he had just gone through and the one that was ahead of him, Harvey suddenly felt hopeful. After all, he told himself, Dante had gone through hell before catching a glimpse of Beatrice. But he was already holding her hand.

Chapter Twelve

Breaking the Law

She counts the days on the calendar. She has no choice. She knows she should call to confirm her appointment, but she's too jittery. She unfolds her still lean body, walks to the closet and drags out her khaki jacket, which has seen better days, days that she can barely remember. When she reaches into the pocket where she stores her money, she finds that it's empty. She rifles through all the other pockets, but they're empty, too. She quickly tries to calculate what she's done with the alimony.

Unable to come up with an answer or even the right question, she sits down on the floor and watches the way the light penetrates the dirt-streaked living room windows forming a pool on the faded fake Persian carpet. Somehow the light's persistence encourages her.

She walks back into the kitchen overrun with dirty dishes and empties the contents of three drawers onto the linoleum floor. Then she gets down on her hands and knees and picks through the assorted debris—several half-used candles, rubber bands, pieces of aluminum foil, scraps of paper, unopened bottles of vitamins, empty prescription bottles, newspaper articles, read and unread, candy wrappers. Finally, she scavenges three dollars in change. Enough to get her where she's going—but nowhere enough to get her where she has to go. Leaving the rest of the mess on the floor, she scurries out of the house.

Sitting on the El, she forgets where she's going and why. After a moment, she tells herself, "Get off at Congress."

"What?" the young woman sitting next to her asks.

"Nothing," she answers. Then asks if she should get off at Congress if she's going to Grant Park. She knows the answer.

"Yeah, going to the demonstration?"

Sabina nods and wonders when she should leave the park in order to get back home in time.

"I'm Janet," the black woman sitting next to her says. "You look kind of familiar."

Sabina looks at Janet. But she doesn't quite see her.

"Were you in Suzanne Kaplan's Lit class last year?"

"Maybe." As soon as she says it, Sabina knows she sounds idiotic and wishes she could take it back. Wishes she were wearing her hooded black sweater so she could hide inside of it, erasing her identity. She sees Janet give her a look and slides closer to the window. "Pynchon," she says to Janet.

Janet doesn't respond.

"We read Pynchon in the class."

"Yeah."

"Couldn't actually get there very often. But I liked it. The instructor—or whatever. Mysterious. The book."

When they get to their stop, Sabina slowly unfolds and rises. Janet pushes past her and empties out of the train before Sabina reaches the door. By the time she climbs the stairs to ground level, Sabina wants to turn around, head home and find a way to numb her brain. But some primal instinct pushes her towards the park. She wanders around in a daze. Feeling battered by the crush of thousands of demonstrators. Preoccupied by her own private battle.

Time evaporates. Hours, maybe days later, maybe just minutes later, she isn't sure—she's caught in a rush of blue undulating towards her. I'm drowning, she thinks. And she tries to swim out of the park. But she forgets how to move.

"Hey! Hey!" someone yells at her.

She turns around.

"Hey," she hears again. "Girl from the El—from Suzanne Kaplan's class . . ."

Sabina tries to focus.

"Did you take something?"

Sabina stares at her.

"Are you on something? Tripping?"

"No," she says. But wishes she were.

"You can't just stand there. We gotta get out of here."

The black girl mumbles something about someone named Becky; then says, "Oh never mind."

Just then a guy explodes in front of them. Red blood hurls out of his head and dances in the air. She doesn't realize it's just his long, wild red hair. Doesn't know that hours later, his head will, in fact, explode.

Janet grabs Sabina's arm and drags her along, zigzagging towards Michigan Avenue.

Minutes later, they fling themselves into a crowd of demonstrators heading in the same direction.

"What time is it?" Sabina asks, anxiously.

Janet checks her watch. "Four. Almost four o'clock."

Sabina groans, remembering her seven o'clock appointment. "It's now or never," she says, more to herself than to Janet.

"Yeah, well," Janet says. And Sabina sees that Janet's shaking. "What were you doing—just standing there, girl?"

159

"All the blood. Makes my knees turn to rubber."

"Blood? Someone's head got busted?"

"Maybe not."

Before they hit the street, Sabina feels that the panic in the park has subsided. But she doesn't trust her instincts anymore. Then she hears Janet giggle.

"What the hell," Janet says. "We're safe."

Sabina and Janet try to slow down their breathing. But now that the adrenalin of panic has been unleashed, Sabina has no control over her body, and she exhales in staccato bursts. She spots her childhood friend, Brad and his wife, whose name she can't remember, and looks down so they won't recognize her. Appropriate. She can't recognize herself.

Janet giggles again, and Sabina feels disoriented. "Gotta go," she says. She compels her legs to carry her out of the park, even though she'd feel safer crawling.

When she gets home, she empties out the drawers in the bedroom. But she still can't come up with enough money. She wanders back to the kitchen, looks through the mess on the floor again, looks up at the wall phone, then empties out a cabinet. Still no cash. Finally, with more determination than she's shown in weeks, she picks up the phone and dials her parents' number. She hangs up, not trusting to luck. Then dials her father's store.

"Berman's Shoes," he says, with a slight Eastern European accent. It always shocks her to hear her father's voice over the phone. In person, she usually doesn't hear the accent, but over the phone the contours of his face, blurred by time, morphs into an amalgam of others faces. She listens to him as if he were a stranger.

"Berman's Shoes," he repeats.

"Daddy," she whispers, half choking on the word.

There's a long silence. She can hear him breathing on the other end of the line. He inhales a cigarette, then exhales. He'd been told to stop smoking years ago.

"You all right, Sabina?"

She tries to answer. But she can't. She knows if she even attempts to open her mouth again, grief will pour into the phone and electrocute her father on the other end.

"Binnie?" he asks, calling her by the nickname no one ever uses anymore.

She closes her eyes and puts the phone back on the hook; then she returns to the living room and watches the sunlight slowly disappear.

She hears him pull up in front of her house. The blue Chevy sedan, old-fashioned even before he brought it home from the dealer, slides to the curb with an audible sigh. He gets out, coughs a few times; then slams the car door shut. She hears him run up the grey, rotting, wooden porch steps, almost tripping. She hears him stamp out his cigarette before he knocks on the door. She sits there, motionless. He walks to the dirt-streaked window, puts his hand on the glass and peers in. Seeing her, he points towards the door.

Like a zombie, she gets up and walks to the hallway, brushing against the coat rack laden with the ghosts of old sweaters whose inhabitants had long ago disappeared. She ignores the musty smell, opens the door, and lets her father into her life.

The small-boned man, bent more from sorrow than fatigue or old age, and the taller young woman, coming apart at the edges, stand looking at each other. Like a father who's been gone for a long time and has returned to find that his child has grown up without him. Both are sorry, but they can't make up for the lost time that stretches between them.

Finally, he makes a move. Tentatively, he puts his arms around her and strokes her long, limp, chestnut-colored hair, as he used to when she was a little girl and had fallen and hurt herself. It's always been this way, she thinks.

The touch of his hand on her hair conveys more tenderness and love than she's felt for months. She buries her face in his shoulder and begins to sob, wrenching out hidden feelings of lost hope and broken promises.

She'd never told her parents, because they'd never wanted to know. They saw her children, of course, but her mother refused to come to her house after they left. By mutual, unspoken agreement, Sabina and her parents had drifted apart. Sabina and her father saw one another now and then, and he slipped her money when he thought she needed it, but she knew he didn't want to actually acknowledge that she had any "real" problems. He preferred to go along with her mother.

Sabina tries not to think about her mother, but she can't help herself. She remembers the last time she saw her. "You're a selfish girl, Sabina," her mother said. "No wonder Frank took the children. Even Rose's daughter-in-law—the colored girl—takes care of her child."

When the sobbing finally tapers off, she realizes her father's shirt is soaked.

"I'm sorry," she says, running her hand down his white cotton shirt with its button-down collar, the kind he's worn to work every day for the past 30 years.

"Don't worry. Salt is good to take out the stains."

"Dad . . ."

"I'm here," he says. "But first, could we sit?"

Sabina leads him into the living room and pushes aside a pile of books so he can sit down on the old couch, draped with what once had been a colorful Indian bedspread. Faded by the sunlight, it covers torn spots and material worn thin from years of abuse. The bedspread, still smelling of spices from the Far East, lends an exotic feel to the room filled with mismatched furniture bought at Good Will. Despite her circumstances, Sabina still has an eye for beauty. And even at her lowest point, she'd somehow been able to coax the room into an almost artistic whole. She'd finagled a chair from a second hand shop, walked home with a globe a neighbor was trying to sell, and made a table from a huge spool for wire left in her alley. Still, she wishes at that moment, that she could be like the children of her parents' friends, if not for her sake, then, at least, for her father's.

"I've made a mess of things."

"But you always remember my birthday and Father's Day," he says, quickly.

It's so ludicrous, it makes her laugh.

"If I did, I'm glad."

"People make mistakes. We all make them."

"It's more than a few mistakes, you know. I don't have anyone else to turn to."

"It's right that you should call me."

"Your hair is grey."

"From old age—or maybe worry."

"Or maybe worry," she repeats, echoing him.

"I just didn't know what to do," he says, sadly. "If I say something, will I make it worse? Maybe it's not as bad as I think it is, I tell myself."

"I'm not blaming you."

Looking away, Sabina nervously runs her finger back and forth across the fine scar separating her left eyebrow into neat halves.

"Everybody's descent is different," she says slowly, feeling her way into unfamiliar territory, "but I guess we all wind up the same way—at the bottom of the barrel, and we just keep on going until we're there—and that's it—we're at the bottom. And there's no place else to go."

"But up. You can go up from there."

She wishes she could hold onto the hope in his voice and keep it inside of her for just a moment, so she can remember what it feels like.

"Maybe."

"You need my help, you got my help," he says, without really looking at her.

"I want you to know . . ."

"I don't have to know. You ask me for help, and I give it to you because I'm your father."

"I want to tell you."

"Do you need money? If you need money, I have it for you. Take it," he says, reaching into his pocket and pulling out his wallet.

He hands her three one hundred dollar bills.

"How did you know?"

"A growing girl always needs money. Take it. Take it."

"I need money so I can . . ."

"Buy yourself a lipstick, some clothes, whatever. You're a smart girl, Binnie, the smartest in your class. You're still young. You can still make something out of your life."

"I have to see a doctor later."

"Good. It's good you're finally taking care of yourself. You look too thin. Next time I come, I'll bring chocolates."

Her father reaches into his pocket again. "I'll leave you the keys. I'll get the car tomorrow."

"I'm scared."

"Everybody's afraid to go to the doctor," her father says, quickly.

"These days you could have a million different things and not know it." He puts the car keys in her hand.

"Remember the pink Caddy?" she asks, suddenly.

"Yeah," he sighs. "That was a car."

"Where'd you get the money you just gave me?"

"Robbed a bank."

"Gambling? That's how you got the Caddy, isn't it?"

"How I lost it, too."

"I thought mom made you sell it."

"Sarah? Nah. Sabina, don't blame her for everything. She does what she can."

He pauses for a long moment in mid-decision. "The money's from her," he says, finally.

Sabina refuses the information. She hands the keys back to her father. "My friend said she'd drive me."

"Okay, then. Okay," he says, with obvious relief. He clearly loves the girl, but he's already overburdened by the vicissitudes of his own life.

Sabina fingers the money and feels angry—angry because she has to take it from him—and from her mother. Angry because he's bought her off so easily. Angry because he's dammed up her insides to prevent the real catharsis, the flood which he knew was coming but which had frightened him so much that he'd stuck his finger in the dike to stop the flood.

Angry at herself because she knows that if she'd had a choice, she would have chosen the money over the confession, anyway.

"Cash in advance," Naomi says, as they walk towards her brand new 1968 Oldsmobile. "That's what they all want. At least, you found a real doctor." She gathers up her red and yellow print, ankle-length diaphanous cotton skirt, brought at the Mexican shop on Dempster, and slides into the driver's seat.

Sabina, now dressed in a similar skirt, doesn't respond.

"I went with my sister—to some dump on the south side. Tell you what—I don't know who was more scared, her or me. You feel like you're committing some crime, or something."

"It is a crime."

"Okay. So maybe it is. Don't worry; you'll be fine," Naomi says, as she reaches over and turns on the car radio.

"Fuckin' A," she shouts as soon as the news comes on to round out the hour. "It was bad down there today."

"Where?" Sabina asks, as she bends down to buckle her sandals.

"Jesus, Sabina. You used to be right up there on the front lines. The demonstration at Grant Park."

In the recesses of her mind, Sabina remembers wandering through the park just a few hours ago. Remembers the explosion of blood. She gags, afraid to think about her appointment. More blood. She thinks about the black girl from lit class. What book were we talking about, she wonders. "I was there," she says.

"Okay. I know this isn't easy for you."

"Pynchon," she says suddenly.

"Pinchin' who?"

"Thomas Pynchon. Wrote a book I was reading for my lit class," Sabina says. "Never finished it." She chalks that up to another thing she'd planned to do that never got done. She vaguely wonders why time, now that she has so much of it on her hands, has closed in on her and kept her static, rather than allowing her to expand. When Jesse and Marty lived with her,

166

she'd been able to do three or four things at once. She amends that to: when Jesse and Marty lived with me before I began ingesting those little magic pills so I could dance with the devil.

Yeah, she thinks. We'd been inseparable for months—me and the good lady in white. The heavenly nurse who came to administer the healing as soon as Sabina pushed the call button. She did everything for Sabina, and in return Sabina was totally dedicated to her. She became the focal point of Sabina's life, replacing the need for food, sleep, sex, and even love. And sometimes long into the night, she felt as if she were on the verge of a real breakthrough, a real understanding of something profound. At times, she felt as if she were getting closer and closer to "it." But then she'd forget exactly what the "it" was that she was pursuing. So she'd pick up one of the books strewn around her room and begin reading, starting sometimes in the middle, sometimes at the end. She'd finish in erratic spurts. And if the book gave her some clue, she'd start at the beginning. If not, she'd toss it aside.

She'd thought she was on a roll then, though occasionally she realized that on some level, she knew she'd essentially checked out of her children's lives.

Sabina cringes as she glances at Naomi, who's concentrating on the road and on the news still blaring out of the radio.

"Shit, Sabina! Did you hear that?"

"What?"

"The cops are still busting heads!"

"The police are chasing demonstrators through Grant Park and across the street to the Hilton Hotel," a disembodied male voice on the radio breathlessly announces.

"Jesus Christ!" Naomi yells.

For the second time that day Sabina, who isn't usually a crier, starts to cry. I should have stayed, she thinks. She cares about the demonstration in Grant Park. She cares about what

167

was happening to her country and to Vietnam. The war has eaten its way into her very being and is irrevocably tied to her personal battles. Though she tries to concentrate on the radio, her mind keeps slipping back to that day—that inevitable day. She has trouble remembering to eat and sleep, has trouble remembering future appointments and past indiscretions, but that particular scenario never changes no matter how many times she replays it.

She's sitting on the floor of the living room, wondering if she could—should—do what the Berrigan brothers, two defrocked Catholic priests, had done. She thinks about Daniel, who'd been arrested last year after the March on Washington, which she has a vague memory of attending. She remembers that while Daniel was in jail, Philip Berrigan and a few other guys poured blood over draft records in the Baltimore Customs House.

Sabina longs to be a Berrigan. If I were a Berrigan, I wouldn't be sitting in Naomi's car on the way to my appointment; I'd be in jail. She wants to be brave, like the Berrigans. She wishes she'd been with them when both brothers walked into the Selective Service office in Catonsville, Maryland, three months ago. I, too, would have emptied all the draft files into a wire basket and napalmed them in the parking lot. When the Berrigans broke the law, they made a heroic choice, she thinks.

Sabina had begun meditating on other choices, as well, on that day she'd been thinking about the Berrigans. And she'd suddenly wondered who'd made the right one, Daedalus or Icarus. When she resurfaced from her meditation, to her great shock, she saw Marty rummaging through her purse.

"What are you doing!"

"I'm hungry, Mom," he said, sheepishly, apologetically. "There's nothing in the house to eat."

Some rational part of her understood his anguished cry. Some part of her remembered that she hadn't cashed the child support check, hadn't bought groceries, hadn't done any of the things mothers do. But the memory seemed stuck on the other side of a tunnel she couldn't quite back into, so she heard herself telling him that "Man does not live by bread alone." She'd been so sure that this was not only brilliant, but correct, because she couldn't remember when she had eaten last. And she'd never felt more fulfilled in her life than she had at that moment.

She'd smiled at Marty. Even now, sitting in Naomi's car, she feels her whole mouth stretching out across her face. She'd felt ecstatic then, so she was surprised when tears began filling his eyes and rolling down his cheeks.

"Let's go for a run," she said. "Come on. It'll make you feel better."

She took off and sped through the house, out the front door, leaving it open so Marty could follow her. When she turned around to say something to him a few blocks later, she noticed that he wasn't there, but she couldn't stop running. It made her feel so good. It made her feel like Icarus. If she just stayed on course and didn't fly too close to the sun, she'd make it.

She was barely winded when she got home and was almost happy to see Frank's car in front of the house. But as soon as she walked through the doorway, he began spewing out the kind of venom she thought was reserved for rapists and murders. For a moment, she had no idea why he was so angry. Then her head cleared, and with complete clarity, she saw herself as Frank saw her. And she was not only ashamed, she was terrified.

"When you want help, give me a call. I'll see what I can do," he said finally.

169

Though Sabina could sometimes accept help, she'd never been able to ask for it. She didn't want help then. She didn't need help. But as long as he stood there glaring at her, she couldn't shake the fear running up and down her spine. She believed that if she remained perfectly still and willed it, her body would disappear from the room and leave only electricity. Then she could return as her real self, her old self. And he wouldn't look at her that way.

"I'm taking the kids with me. Do you hear me?"

She didn't answer because she didn't want to break the spell.

Though the heavenly nurse continued to come around after that, she'd lost her power to heal. And Sabina realized that she'd flown way too close to the sun. Her wings had melted along with whatever sense of self still remained.

Sabina shakes her head. She doesn't want to think anymore. She needs to tell Naomi to turn the car around and head back downtown to Grant Park. Russell Means and two dozen other Native Americans are occupying the park. No, no, this isn't about Indians. Hang on. Hang on. Someone on the radio just mentioned Vietnam. Vietnam! Grant Park. The humongous teach-in. She was there. But that was another day.

Naomi settles into a chair in the waiting room and gobbles up "Time Magazine" as Sabina grows agitated, picking at her cuticles. Like most medical offices, the waiting room is modern, spare, and serviceable, with bland art any Sunday painter could have contributed, positioned evenly on the walls. It's after hours, so Sabina is the only patient; even the receptionist has left.

Doctor Siegel's nurse, whose brisk manner immediately makes Sabina even more nervous, finally ushers her into an examining room, which is ice cold. Peeling off her clothes, as she'd been instructed to do, Sabina shivers.

"Doctor will be here in a few minutes," the nurse says.

Sabina lies down on the narrow table and covers herself with a sheet. A pale blue sheet, the same color as the medical equipment and the walls.

The nurse plunges an IV into Sabina's arm and begins a morphine drip. "It'll only take a few minutes. Then it'll be all over. It'll just feel like a bad cramp."

"It'll hurt," Sabina says as the nurse leaves the room. She tells herself not to be scared and wonders if she's said it out loud.

Maybe I shouldn't do it, she thinks suddenly. I can change my mind. It's not too late. After all, Jesse and Marty were angelic children. Because of me? Or despite me? She laughs, suddenly feeling light-headed. There are no accidents, she thinks. It must mean something. If the other two were angels, maybe this one was—no—I can't go there. But why not? Let me think; let me think. The father. Oh god, who's the father? Her mind races; she can't remember. Then suddenly, it comes to her. The bar in Old Town. The big guy with dark, wavy hair. Funny guy. Smart. A writer. A writer for the "Sun-Times." Having a drink with James Joyce. No, maybe not. Has to be. Can't remember anyone else. I'd be a better mother this time; I won't abandon this one. I didn't really abandon Jesse and Martin; I just got confused.

She's afraid this is her last chance. She's afraid if she lets this baby go, her whole life will fall apart. There will be nothing to anchor her. She's afraid she'll simply float away—but she doesn't know how she will support the child.

"God will provide," she hears a far off voice say.

"Oh right," she answers. "Like he has so far. Provided me with enough LSD to help me cross the border into infinity and come back empty."

No, she thinks. I blew it. When I had the chance, I blew it. Will Jesse and Martin hate me the way I hate my mother? The pieces began to crumble. Maybe she didn't hate her mother. She suddenly thinks of her mother's little life of discomfort, waiting and hoping for her children to provide the satisfaction she could never provide for herself. It's a life of mismatched appetizers without a main course. Sabina is filled with regret. My mother's saving money for their plots, hers and my father's, and she has no idea they're already dead. If only he'd kept the pink Caddy.

Suddenly, she hears a smattering of conversation outside the consultation room.

I'm not ready yet. She sits up in a panic. But the doctor enters the room.

I'm an unnatural mother. Worse than Medea.

"Okay, slide down a little," the doctor says, without any formalities, not even an introduction. He's dressed in blue to match the office.

I will do the right thing, she thinks.

"Lie still; don't squirm."

That would be the only rational thing to do, but I've never been a rational woman.

My mother always used to say, "Why can't you be like everyone else? Everyone's out of step but Johnny." I always wanted to meet Johnny. I figured we must be soul mates. Only my mother would never tell me where I could find him, so I went looking for him in all the wrong places.

Whatever I choose to do, it will be the wrong decision.

All the books she'd read, all the religion and philosophy—

nothing had prepared her for this. They'd prepared her in the abstract, and in the abstract, there was only one possible choice. But there was a whisper inside of her that didn't come from books, and as she lay there, it was becoming more and more insistent. She tried to listen to it. She just needed a little more time to decide whether or not she could trust that voice. She wanted to. But after all, it was the same voice that had whispered to her before, wrapping itself around her, dancing the dance of the seven veils, enticing her to follow the Pied Piper to oblivion, and to an unexpurgated happiness.

"All done," the doctor says, as he gathers up his tools.

She lies there, feeling empty and deprived. Then she looks out of the window and sees a sliver of moon tipping in her direction. It holds the promise of fulfillment. I've made my own heroic choice, she thinks. I've broken the law. I'll strap on a pair of sturdier wings. I'll rejoin the movement. I'll find the Berrigans.

Chapter Thirteen

Almost

How come you ask me why I'm so tough? Why not strong? It's not a choice. If I weren't tough, I'd probably be dead by now."

"Elizabeth mentioned where you grew up."

"Yeah. Well. I have to go find Becky. Tell her I can't locate a medic."

"I'll walk back to the Band Shell with you."

"Still think I'll protect you, huh?"

"Yep."

"You're a white boy. You don't need protection. Cops aren't gonna shoot you in the head and call you the aggressor."

"What is it with you? White boy this and white boy that?"

"You are a white boy."

"Yeah. I'm a white boy. Do I go around calling you a black girl?"

"Probably do. Behind my back."

"Jesus, you're cynical."

"Yeah. Or maybe you're thinking paranoid."

"You angry at me 'cause I'm white? Or you angry with me for some other reason?"

"Who says I'm angry at chu? World doesn't revolve around you, you know."

"What more do I have to do to prove myself?"

"What more? In other words—I married a black chick. I don't gotta do nothin' else."

"I don't care what the hell color she is; she could be purple, for all I care."

"Ah. That's sweet. Like, whoa, look at me. I got this black girl by my side—proof of my commitment to the cause."

"Not what I meant, Janet. Not why I married Elizabeth."

"Yeah? Be honest. Isn't that just a little part of it?"

"No."

"You answered too quickly."

"And you jumped on me too quickly."

"Elizabeth ever tell you where she grew up?"

"Evanston."

"Before that."

Brad stops walking and looks at Janet. "Before that?"

"Yeah, white boy. Before she and her mom moved to Evanston."

"I— I . . ."

"Came up in the same damn ghetto I did. Till she left."

"When did she move to Evanston?"

"Ask her, big boy. Surprised she never mentioned it."

"Yeah," he says softly. Not sure she's telling the truth and not sure what it means if she is.

"Jesus, hard to believe so many people showed up."

"I don't think you're gonna find Becky."

"Probably not."

"What was it like?" he asks, shuttling between his emotions.

"What was what like?" she asks, knowing exactly what he means.

"Living there."

"Like hell. No. Wrong. It wasn't like hell. It was hell. Still is."

"When I was growing up, I—you know—I never knew anyone who lived there."

"Not sure you could exactly call it living, man."

"There were black kids at my high school."

"Ah huh."

"Okay, so not too many were in my classes."

"Yeah, I bet."

"Look, I can't help where I grew up any more than you can help where you grew up. Wasn't a choice. Kids go to school, come home from school, do their homework, play ball with the other kids in the neighborhood, then go to bed and dream about growing up and playing baseball for the White Sox or if they're really lucky, the Cubs. Sometimes we manage to venture outside the neighborhood—but never alone. And we make a lot of noise, so no one will know we're nervous. We get down and dirty with the Italian kids and don't tell our parents where we're going, cause they'd freak out. And it feels dangerous. Good dangerous. Then one day this black kid in my art class invites me to his house and tells me where he lives. Kind of as a dare, I think. Like this white boy ain't never gonna come over to my side of town. And I go. I ride my bike. It's not that far from where I live, but it might as well be on another planet. I'm scared, but I'll be damned if I'm gonna turn back. And I find his street. More like an alley. And this little house—a shack with peeling paint and a few boarded up windows. There's an old beat-up truck on the front lawn. The front door's open. 'Hey, Willie,' I call, cause I'm afraid to go up to the door, and I'm afraid if I leave my bike it won't be there when I come back down the front steps. And I'll be stranded there forever. Willie comes out and looks at me like he's not the least bit surprised that I'm there, even though I am. He's holding a beer bottle in his hand, and he nods for me to come in. I drag my bike onto the front porch. He snickers. I want to go home, but I go in anyway. It's dark inside. At least, that's the way I remember it. Not really dark, but there's no light coming in through the windows. And this woman's sitting at a table in the middle of the living room. It's kind of a kitchen table of some sort. And there's no other furniture in the room. Or, at least, I don't remember any. She's drinking a beer, too. She's a white woman. And she's drunk. I can tell by the way she talks and the way she looks at me. I feel like I'm in some kind of dream. I don't feel the weight of my body. Willie offers me a beer. 'I'm driving,' I say nervously, hoping he'll think it's funny. He doesn't laugh. I don't know how to act. I don't know how to leave without hurting his feelings, but he's just smiling his smile at me. The white woman says, "Hey, there," so I have to look at her. I'm wondering what she's doing in this house, looking like she belongs but doesn't belong. There's sweat on her upper lip and a dark stain between her breasts where her blue T-shirt forms little tents around her nipples. She squeezes her breast and winks at me. "Hey," I say, my voice cracking. She smells my discomfort. I stay a few minutes longer. Then the next day at school, it's like it never happened. We don't even say hello. Me and Willie. You understand, it's . . ."

"Shut the fuck up, Brad. I'm fucking sick of this conversation."

Brad reels—his mouth suspended in mid flight.

"Stop playing the good guy. Mr. Fucking Good Guy."

"I'm not playing the good guy."

"Then what the hell are you playing? Why you telling me that story that don't mean shit? I grew up in the ghetto, man; we know how to play the doubles in more ways than one. Talk one way to your own people and another way to white folks. Dazzle them with your convoluted logic so they're confused about what the hell you mean, but they're afraid to ask because they don't want to look stupid—more stupid than some stupid black kid. And you know why? You wanna know why we do that? To keep Mr. Whitey in the dark. So he won't know shit about our business. Any of our business. Even if he thinks he does."

"I don't understand what's happening here. You're Elizabeth's friend. I thought you were my friend, and you fucking attack me, like I'm Richard Fucking Nixon. I am not the enemy, Janet. Get that through your head. Or maybe you already know that. Maybe I should be grateful that you're not double talking me—that you're not treating me like the other white folks."

"Got you a point there, white boy."

"Good."

"Just one."

"What's bugging you, anyway?"

"Nothing."

"Hate to run into you when something is." He laughs from the throat up, constricted.

"How come she never told you?"

He hesitates for a moment. Anything he says might seem like a betrayal. "What difference does it make?" he finally answers.

"Oh Jew boy. Always answering a question with a question."

He blanches. "Do we?'

She laughs a deep throaty laugh.

"We have our own ghettoes, you know. Maybe that's our version of double talk."

Suddenly, demonstrators nearby start screaming and running towards them. They spot the cops closing in from every direction. No time to ask what's going on.

"Run, Jew boy," she cries.

They sprint towards the street, trying to escape the known and the unknown.

They slide into a booth at the Artists' Café across the street. Her thighs feel hot against the red leather seats. She takes a swipe at the puddle of sweat between her breasts and remembers walking past the window one day on her way to Roosevelt and seeing a guy sitting in this same booth. One bare foot propped up on the table. His fork between his big toe and the one next to it. The sight was so disorientating that it didn't seem real. He smiled at her. Her mouth automatically moved to return the smile, though she had no memory in that moment of where she was or why she was there, or if she'd suddenly been transported to outer space on a drug trip sponsored by the Chamber of Commerce. By the time she got to the corner, she was convinced that she hadn't actually seen what she thought she saw. She has that same feeling now and half expects the guy to materialize and sit across the table from her.

Brad takes a napkin and wipes his leaking forehead. He puts his hand on his heart as if that will stop the pounding—and the fear.

"Don't call me Jew boy."

"Why not?"

Brad believes totally in non-violence. But at that moment, he feels like reaching over and smacking Janet across her lovely black face, wiping the smile off of her honey-colored lips, leaving a big red handprint on her skin, seeing tears run out of her eyes and settle in the shafts of her long, curly lashes.

He takes a deep breath and settles back against the booth, his teeth grinding in angry rotation.

"You embarrassed about being a Jew? Maybe I mean it as a compliment."

"You want me to call you black girl?"

"Sure. Why not? Depends on the way you say it. You could say 'Hey, black girl' and mean bitch. Or you could say 'Hey, black girl' and mean you are hot. Or you are cool. Or don't you even look at that sweater; just march your ass out of this here department store."

"Yeah."

"Yeah what?"

"Maybe I am embarrassed. When I was in kindergarten, there weren't many Jews in our neighborhood. The Catholic school was across the street. Our playgrounds faced each other, and every day, I'd stand at the fence and wave to my friend Jerry McKenzie who lived down the block from me. And every day, the kids at the Catholic school would yell, "Christ killer." Until I was in fourth grade, I had no idea they were yelling it at me."

Janet laughs. "Think of it this way, white boy, you can pass if you want to. Blond hair. Green eyes. Me—I ain't ever gonna pass for anything other than a black girl."

"A beautiful black girl," he says softly.

"You mean the term generically or for real?"

He looks at her swollen lips that contain untold memories and at her narrow nose that indicates a violation somewhere in her history.

"For real."

She allows herself to see him for the first time; then gets up from the table and slides into the booth next to him. "Truce," she says, extending her hand.

Neither of them will admit that a rush of hot confusion has taken their bodies captive.

In the midst of the embarrassment, Janet stammers. "She didn't even say good-bye."

He somehow knows what she means.

"She was there one day. And gone the next. Like she suddenly evaporated. And then there she was sitting two seats away from me in my Lit class."

"I'm sorry."

"Wasn't you who did it. Wanna get out of here?"

"Yeah. I should be heading home."

They both know that's not what either of them have in mind. Brad glances at the bill and leaves some money on the table. They get up in a trance and walk slowly to the door, the heat between their bodies palpable.

The Poor People's Campaign is marching past them—up Michigan Avenue. Janet spots Becky in a line of demonstrators behind the mule train. She turns away. She wants what's due.

They stand there for a moment as the light turns red. The mule train stops. Brad breathes in Abernathy's sense of determination. He thinks that Abernathy emanates a kind of purity, the same kind of purity he sees in Elizabeth.

"I should be heading home," he says. He smiles. She cocks her head and looks at him for a long moment.

"Yeah. Elizabeth will be worrying about you."

He leans down and kisses her hot cheek. Then walks quickly to the corner and heads towards State Street.

Chapter Fourteen

Hell No, We Won't Go

Julian could fool everyone except his mother. Almost everyone. He couldn't fool his sister Kari, either. That bothered him sometimes. Not the fact that he couldn't fool his mother or his sister. The fact that he could fool just about everyone else. Julian had eased his way through high school using a combination of Cliffs' Notes and charm.

He'd make himself comfortable, sitting on the edge of teachers' desks, looking right into their eyes, engaging in what passed for deep conversation. "I love 'Othello,'" he'd said to his English teacher, a ruddy-faced, middle-aged woman who wore lace-up shoes with clunky heels like his grandmother. And who'd stopped expecting much from her students years ago.

"Really?" she asked. More as a statement than a question. She looked up from the paper she was grading, which coincidentally had Julian's name on it. "I'm delighted to hear you say that, Julian. Lots of students complain about having to study Shakespeare."

"Yeah, I know. But he was a very cool dude. Tough but ya know, soft-hearted underneath."

"Soft headed, too. At least, when it came to jealousy." Miss Murray chuckled. A little wickedly, Julian thought.

"So why did he believe Iago? I mean, come on, anyone

could see the dude was a liar." Julian picked up a small grey and white glass bear Miss Murray kept on her desk.

"Good question. But we know things about Iago that Othello didn't. So we have an advantage."

"Yeah, well . . ."

"Yeah, well, unfortunately, some people are very good liars." She took off her horn-rimmed glasses, turned her head to the side, and studied Julian.

Julian flashed a dimpled grin, hoping to disarm her. Nah, he thought, she doesn't mean me. Yes, she does, a little voice said. A quiet voice that he usually chose to ignore. I'm not exactly a liar, he thought. Maybe a pretender. Makes life a lot easier.

He put the glass bear back on the desk.

Miss Murray slid it a quarter of an inch to the side; then she put her glasses back on and looked at Julian again. "We know the consequences for Othello and Desdemona. But I keep wondering if, in a universe beyond the play, the Iagos of the world also pay a price."

For some reason, Julian thought about his conversation with Miss Murray as he was waking up. Maybe it was the dream I had last night that triggered it. The dream. Where did it go? Remembered it two minutes ago. Can't remember one thing about it now. Only that I woke up feeling like my head was screwed on backwards.

"Julian. Time to get up, lock and load."

"Fuck." He looked up at his high school buddy Quinn who was shaking him. Harder than he needed to. It bothered him for a moment; then he thought, what the hell? Quinn's Quinn. No reason to make an issue out of it. He looked around the armory that had been transformed into a quasi-military barracks. All the weekend warriors were tumbling out of their cots. Groaning. Burping. Farting. It was like summer camp. Only it wasn't.

Julian lumbered into the communal bathroom and took a long, soulful piss. After which he bleated like a goat in heat. Then he ran his hand under the dripping faucet and wiped it on his military issue boxer shorts.

On his way out the door, he glanced at Craig Anderson standing in front of the mirror inspecting his clipped hair cut. Julian would have snickered if he were the snickering type. But he wasn't. So he just smiled. He'd run into Anderson on Rush Street a while ago. The guy had had a Paul McCartney do. Whoa, he'd thought, how'd he get it to grow so fast? Wasn't hanging below his helmet the week before last. "Hey, Anderson," he'd said. He was about to ask Anderson what kind of fertilizer he used on his head—then he realized that Anderson was wearing a wig.

"I'm in the advertising business, dude. Can't go around looking like a red neck."

Unlike Anderson, Julian didn't seem to care about the way he looked. He'd often forget to shave, and a blond stubbly beard would appear. Being Julian, the stubble didn't hide his beauty, it enhanced it in a modest, humble sort of way that he didn't quite recognize but used to his advantage, anyway. One of his mother's friends called him Thor. He made the hearts of older women, including his father's secretary, go pitter-patter. But he took it in stride. They loved him even more for his endearing sense of humor and little boyishness. People like taking care of me, Julian thought. So I let them.

Like Anderson, Julian also hated getting his shaggy hair cut. Just as it would begin look normal, he'd have to cut it regulation length for the once a month weekend inspection. Every time he went to the barber, he'd think about Samson, the only

Bible story he remembered from Sunday school, and feel his strength peel away with every snip.

When he was out of uniform, Julian wore faded t-shirts with stretched out necks and blue jeans with paint stains on them. Girls stared at him, anyway. And when he did get dressed up in his casual way, he looked as if he were ready to strut down the runway. He knew it. But he also knew how disarming it was to pretend that he didn't.

A talent agent had once stopped him on Michigan Avenue as he was about to cross the street.

"Hello," she said, looking him up and down. Julian was used to that kind of look, so he just smiled at her and was about to walk away when she touched his arm. "I'm a talent agent. If you can talk, I can get you into the movies."

He could talk. He was a natural. But Julian couldn't act. He could only be Julian, which was, maybe, the best act of all. But it wasn't good enough for Hollywood. So after six months of the kind of rejection he wasn't used to, Julian had come back home to Chicago. At the age of nineteen, he was depressed for the first time in his life. Or maybe not the first time. But it seemed like it. He didn't like to remember the other time.

Terrified that his number would be called, he'd decided to join the National Guard with Quinn. Six months active duty. No oversees service. No Vietnam. After he got out, one weekend a month for six years. They thought dressing up like soldiers and playing war games would be a gas.

His six months of pure hell at Fort Leonard Wood Missouri, turned out to be a lot less fun than he'd anticipated. Aside from the usual stress of extreme physical torture, he'd contracted an unholy case of poison ivy that traveled down his entire body, encasing his genitals like a protective crust. Protecting him from what, he didn't know.

The itching was so severe that he wound up in the infirmary, which would have been a relief from the daily hell of marching in the heat with a thirty pound backpack, climbing barriers and slithering across the ground with his weapon if the itching hadn't driven him out of his mind. At least that's what it felt like.

When his six months were over, he enrolled at Roosevelt University for the spring semester.

Except for the weekends when he continued to train with the Guard, Julian had hung around the house after the end of the semester, until his mother had an idea. "If you don't get a job by next week, I'm going to buy some paint and some rollers, and you're going to paint the house. Just get through college; then you can go to law school like everyone else. And you can act in front of a judge."

Instead, Julian finagled a job as a waiter at Jovan, a high-end restaurant, and made a ton of money in tips—even on the night he spilled a glass of water on a grey-haired older man, soaking his perfectly-tailored suit. "Okay," he said, handing the man a steak knife. "Kill me, sir. I deserve it." The man laughed. "You probably do. But get me a few napkins, and we'll forgo the death penalty."

As he waited on other tables, Julian watched the man out of the corner of his eye and wondered about him and his son. Julian assumed the younger man was his son because they looked alike. Except the younger man wore little round glasses with wire frames, like John Lennon's.

When the man and his son finished dinner, Julian brought them a check.

"What the hell do you make teaching at the Art Institute, anyway?" Julian heard the father ask.

He put the silver tray containing the tab on the table.

John Lennon-look-alike just laughed at the question. Doesn't seem like the arty type, Julian thought. Maybe teachers are different from real artists.

As the two men walked out of the restaurant, Julian picked up the bill and noted that the old man had left him a forty-dollar tip.

Julian and Quinn wandered into the temporary mess hall. Julian looked at the S.O.S. being ladled onto plates and wished he were in his mother's sun-filled kitchen sitting at the white Formica table next to his sister Kari. Kari was two years older than Julian and not nearly as pretty. But what she lacked in beauty, she made up for in more subtle ways.

Julian and Quinn sat down at a long aluminum table with their re-constituted eggs, burnt toast and undrinkable coffee.

"I didn't sign up for this shit, man," Julian groused.

"You didn't read the fine print, boyo. They can call us up in an emergency. Any time they want."

Julian propped up his long legs on the bench across from him. "I think my sister was there last night. Said she was going with Father Donley."

"The dude lugging a twelve-foot cross through the park?"

"Yeah. When I told her I got called in, she went nuts." Julian began shoveling food into his mouth.

Quinn laughed. "How about driving that jeep, man? Kind of fun, huh?"

"Yeah, kind of." Never admit that to Kari, he thought. Loved trolling around, though. Like I was steering a dodgem car. "But I didn't want to hit anybody. You?"

"Tried to."

"She tried to get me to stay home yesterday. I didn't ask to be called up I told her. 'Well, what did you think—that you

187

were just gonna have fun? I mean, who in their right mind joins the National Guard?' she said."

"'Dad was in the army,' I told her. She pinched my arm. Hard. 'That was a war of necessity,' she said."

"She fucking pinched your arm?"

"'If rules don't work, you have to get rid of them. Not enforce them!' she yelled. But I got her. Shift too far to the left, and you get the French Revolution, I said."

"Julian, wow, who have you been talking to?"

"Impressed ya, huh?"

"Where'd you hear that?"

"My Social Studies teacher senior year." He laughed. "That's the only thing I remember from all of high school."

Quinn broke a grin. "Mr. Keller. Yeah. He used to say that in our class all the time, too. Whenever things got out of control."

"I don't really want to do this, you know. I didn't want to be in Lincoln Park last night. And I sure as hell don't want to go to Grant Park today."

"Nobody forced you to sign up for war games, ya little communist. You could have enrolled in college straight away when you got back from L.A." "I know, but—what the hell? What's done is done," he said, pretending that the whole fucking experience wasn't some nightmare payback the gods decided to inflict on him. Which was what he usually thought when he found himself in a bad situation. "She said, 'If we run into each other, pretend you don't know me. Because I'm gonna pretend I don't know you.'"

Julian trudged back into the communal bathroom after breakfast, trying to psych himself up for the day he wished were already over. *I can just imagine what it's gonna be like. Standing around all morning. Waiting for the sky to fall. Wish* the sergeant was a woman. A twenty-five-year-old babe, black hair, blue eyes, long lashes. Big tits hanging out of her uniform.

He caught a glimpse of himself in the mirror. "Shit!" He tried brushing his hair back with his fingers. "Shit. They're gonna bust me." He wished he had a pair of scissors so he could snip off the ends of his hair.

As he stared at his image, he caught of glimpse of the dream he hadn't been able to remember when he woke up. He shivered. Shit. The memory faded as quickly as it came. But as he was buttoning himself into the jacket of his uniform, he remembered that Alex was in his dream.

He switched on his little transistor radio to block out the image. "No thousands will come to our city and take over our streets, or city, our convention," he heard Mayor Daley spit out. "Hope you're right, your holiness."

Julian squirmed as his sergeant droned on and on. Lazily, he began to analyze the man facing him. Definitely not a babe.

He couldn't figure out how to reconfigure McCoy into the image of his imaginary sex partner. Regardless of the shirt stretched tightly across McCoy's chest, the barely protruding nipples in no way reminded him of the babe's tits. So he tried on another fantasy, conjuring up his American Lit professor from last semester. She's a babe, he thought. Not a babe babe, but a babe. Something really hot about her. Can't figure out exactly what. Certainly not her small tits. He remembered sitting on her desk after class and peering as far down her blouse as he could without being obvious. She knew. He could tell. Still gave me a C.

"We are part of the first line of defense. That's why we've been called up to respond to this here domestic emergency," Sergeant McCoy said as if he'd spent the early part of the morning memorizing those two lines. Julian was startled out of his fantasy. "There are 7,500 National Guardsman on duty today. We're here to assist the 12,000 policemen and make sure there are no incidents."

Good luck, Julian thought. Some crazy thing's bound to go down. He smiled, remembering the Yippies, who'd held their own nominating convention at the Civic Center a few days ago. They nominated a pig with some weird name—sounds like "pig." But it wasn't. Peg. Pegasus. Pegasus for president. Wonder if the Yippies made bail for Pegasus and the seven guys who were arrested. Maybe they'll show up today. Bring a little humor to the whole weird situation.

At least, I'm not in the army. Jesus, those guys from Fort Hood—all the way up here from Texas, sitting in their tanks. Oh, man, if I had to sit in a sweaty tank, that would really bug me.

By noon, Julian and Quinn were standing in front of the bridge spanning Congress Street. In essence, Quinn was the opposite of Julian: dark and ten pounds over-weight with a slight paunch that at 19 predicted a pregnant belly at 29. They'd been told their line of defense would seal off Grant Park and prevent protestors from crossing the bridge onto Michigan Avenue—in case there was trouble.

Shit, it's fucking hot in this uniform and these boots, Julian thought. His loaded M-14 was weighing down his shoulder. Quinn had a bayonet attached to his rifle. Some guys had grenade launchers. What the hell, somebody could really get hurt here. Julian shifted uncomfortably and suddenly started thinking about Alex again. Sometimes he dreamed about him—like last night. Sometimes they had imaginary conversations.

He'd be sitting in class or just standing around, like he was now, and he'd think about the skinny, red-haired kid. Thick mop hanging over his forehead. Into his eyes. His dimples twinkling mischief.

Sometimes I almost envy the kid, he thought. Then immediately retracted it. Don't want to give the gods or fate or whatever any ideas. Anyway, why would I envy him? Shouldn't it be the other way around? Julian bit his bottom lip. Hard. For as long as he could stand it. An old habit of his from childhood. Curiosity killed the cat, he thought. He moved his tongue over his lip and tasted blood.

He suddenly felt as if a great void had opened up inside of him. He looked at Quinn beseechingly. Penitent to priest. As if Quinn could absolve him. As if anyone could.

I was trying to reach the moon, he thought. Julian swallowed hard. I wish Ford hadn't been so curious.

"See ya latter, alligator" Alex used to whisper.

"After while, crocodile," Julian mouthed. He felt the hollowness in his gut expand. Then he was distracted. Distraction, as always, was the key to Julian's survival and his transformation into the golden talker. Sometimes the weaver of other people's dreams. Sometimes the object.

A guy who looked about his age, maybe a year or two older, walked towards him a bit unsteadily. He was wearing a torn work shirt and dirty jeans. Julian braced himself, holding his position. He noted that the guy was wearing combat boots, unlaced, but clearly army issue. He felt repelled by the stench from the guy's unwashed body and flinched when the guy held out his hand.

He's crazy; he's gonna try something, Julian thought. He gripped his M-14.

"Got any change?"

"Hey, man, move on," Quinn said.

The guy held up two fingers, making a peace sign. As he

drifted off, he said to no one in particular, "Yeah, yeah. You go over there. See what it's like. Then come back here and have people spit at you."

Julian and Quinn exchanged glances. "Nam," Quinn whispered.

Nam, Julian thought. Death. The unwelcome visitor. Looked me right in the eye. Right in the fucking eye. But I didn't recognize him; I was too busy having a good time. And, lucky me, he found someone else. Julian counted up the deaths in the past few months—Martin Luther King in April, Bobby Kennedy in June—all the soldiers in Vietnam. Alex. Why Alex? Alex didn't die this year.

They could hear voices blasting out of megaphones. Probably coming from the Band Shell, Julian thought. But they couldn't hear exactly what anyone was saying. Just a word here and there. Chants: "Hell no; we won't go." Names: Dick Gregory. What the hell was a comedian doing here? Julian wondered.

"Heard there were a shitload of demonstrators in front of the Hilton last night," Quinn said under his breath, keeping his eyes straight ahead. "Came down here after Lincoln Park."

"Glad they let us go back to the armory at midnight. I passed out as soon as I hit the pillow."

Just then, screams broke the calm. Julian looked around trying to see what was going on. Doesn't look good, he thought. People started running and throwing things. For a moment, he was confused. Wasn't sure what side he was on. Didn't know if he was more afraid of getting hurt or of hurting some demonstrator. He felt like crying.

"What the fuck?" he yelled. Get yourself together, he thought. This is part of the game. Just fucking play it.

"Move out of the park," he heard someone with a megaphone yell at the crowd. "If we're teargassed, the whole city will have to be teargassed. If they spill our blood, the whole city will see it."

Julian almost choked on the words "spill" and "blood." But only his gut betrayed his terror. From the outside, he looked totally calm. Like always.

"Hold your positions!" Sergeant McCoy shouted. "Do not allow the demonstrators to leave the park! Repeat! Do not allow the demonstrators to leave the park!"

Julian felt a chill snake up his back. Cool down, man. All you have to do is stand here, he told himself. Then his mind went blank. Just like the other time. And the screams became his mother's screams. But he'd just sat in the car that had rolled down the only steep hill in the flatlands of the Midwest.

A minute later, a wave of bodies rolled towards them. Holding their heads. Limping. Cursing and shouting at the police who were chasing them. Julian startled; then his whole body tensed up. He held his breath for a protracted moment. As if he'd forgotten how to breathe. Demonstrators were so close he could see blood spurting from their foreheads. He could smell their blood. That tinny smell that curdles your stomach. That's so strong you can taste it. He cleared his throat, trying to cough it up. To get rid of it. All of it.

"Hold the line!" McCoy shouted.

Julian continued standing at attention. But his insides were shaking.

"Shit!" a girl screamed. "Let us through."

Julian tried not to look at her.

"She's bleeding, man," a guy yelled. "She might have a concussion, or something."

Julian pressed his rifle tightly against leg. "I . . ."

Quinn shot him a look. Julian stopped talking. The girl and the guy glared at him, disgusted. Then moved on. Looking for a break in the barricade. Julian felt sick to his stomach. His eyes stung from the unshed tears that pressed against his lids.

By dusk, the park was relatively quiet. But Julian's stomach was still roiling. "I don't know, man, it was pretty hard just standing there."

"It's our job, dude," Quinn answered coolly. He leaned back against a tree. "We have to do what we have to do."

"Yeah," Julian said. But it was more a question than an agreement. Trapped between hunger and nausea, he thought about Kari and wondered if she were okay. "Jesus, I hope my sister left before the cops started banging people's heads."

"Kari's smart. She probably left early."

"I don't know, man. She's really committed to this anti-war stuff."

"Look, I'm not a big fan of the war, either, but there's nothing we can do about it. It is what it is."

"Maybe."

"Let's just get through the day."

McCoy assigned them to assist the police guarding Michigan Avenue, near the Hilton Hotel. Julian was glad that the crowd had thinned out. *Maybe Kari's gone home*, he thought. He studied the remaining demonstrators who'd lined up in back of the Poor People's Campaign. Didn't see Kari. They weren't expecting any more trouble, McCoy said. But they wanted to be prepared. Just in case.

Julian couldn't ignore the continual clutch at his stomach and wished he could loosen his belt.

I'm so fucking tired of all this. I'm hot. I want this to be over, so I can go home and take a shower.

McCoy told them to allow the Campaign to move forward. "They got a fucking permit to march to the fucking Convention Center," he spat out. Like it affects him personally, Julian thought. Okay, now I feel really stupid. Who the hell's even running on the Democratic ticket? Jesus, after Bobby Kennedy was murdered, gave up paying attention to the other guys. Can't get the picture of Sirhan Sirhan out of my head. Didn't anybody notice the sleazy-looking son-of-a-bitch? When he thought about Bobby Kennedy, the killer's image was always the first Julian saw in his imagination; followed by the one of Kennedy lying on the kitchen floor of the Ambassador Hotel.

That death wasn't an accident, he thought, sadly.

Standing with the heels of his boots smack against the curb, Julian casually wondered what kept him and Kari from being closer. Could guess why, he thought. But as soon as he thought it, he stuffed it. Still, part of him wished he could erase the shield of separation between them. It was always there and not there at the same time. Their dirty little secret, that wasn't even a secret.

The light turned red. The donkey cart pulled to a halt in front of Julian and Quinn. The old guy in the black suit must be boiling, Julian thought. He wanted to swipe his own forehead where trickles of sweat gathered under his helmet.

When the light turned green, the donkey cart crossed to the other side. A few white demonstrators crossed with them. Then the light turned red. And a police squad quickly lined up across Michigan Avenue. "Back 'em up," McCoy yelled. Julian and Quinn stepped into place. The white demonstrators look shocked, Julian thought. He didn't know quite what to expect, either. The light turned green again. The demonstrators tried to cut around the police. But the cops formed a solid wall. The National Guard was right behind them. Exactly where I don't want to be. He could feel the raw mutual hatred between the cops and the demonstrators. *I don't think a smile's not gonna get me through this one.*

A demonstrator caught his eye—a girl with black curly hair. She looked vaguely familiar. She stood next to a tall guy dressed in black and wearing rimless glasses. Julian was trying not to make eye contact with anyone. But something about the girl reminded him of Kari. *No, it's not that. She was in my Lit class last semester,* he remembered. He wanted to warn her to get out while she could. The guy started moving away. He looked familiar, too. But she stayed in line where she was. *Go back,* he wanted to yell.

Then hell erupted.

A soldier in front of the Hilton Hotel started beating up a demonstrator. The crowd shouted for him to stop. But the soldier just kept going. The police did nothing to stop him. Julian was stunned. He glanced at Quinn. Quinn stood eerily still. *He looks like a fucking store dummy. Like he has no idea what's going on over there. What are we supposed to do?* He thought about trying to locate McCoy. Then nixed the idea.

"The pigs are whores. The pigs are whores," the crowd started chanting. "The pigs are whores."

Suddenly, someone threw a Coke bottle at a policeman close to where Julian was standing. The cop went ballistic. Started beating the kid in front of him. Kicking him in the gut. Another cop was nearly hit. He retaliated. Clubbed the demonstrator in front of him. Coming down as hard as he could on the guy's shoulder. Julian winced. But he continued standing at attention. *It doesn't feel real,* he thought. *I'm seeing it right in front of my eyes, but it doesn't feel like I'm really here. Doesn't feel like I'm in my body.*

Then everything seemed to happen at once. *Keep your*

positions!" McCoy shouted. "Do not let anyone cross the street!"

Julian snapped into the moment. All his synapses ignited. He was scared. For himself. And for the demonstrators. In a flash, the feeling he dreaded most rose up to haunt him—here—where he least expected it. The fear was familiar. It was a constant faintly recognizable part of him that he always managed to shove away. Not now, he thought. They're throwing anything they can get their hands on. Shit! They're aiming directly at the police. Stupid. Jesus, the cops don't care who they pound. He looked for the girl from his class and the tall guy with the rimless glasses. Cool down, he wanted to shout at the cops. But even if he could have shouted, no one would have listened.

People in business suits were streaming out of the Hilton Hotel to see what was going on. But the cops were on a roll. And started pounding them, too. Curiosity killed the cat, he thought. Then wondered at the stray idea that momentarily overrode his feeling of helplessness. He glanced at Quinn. Quinn stared straight ahead. Julian looked at the demonstrators again. The dark, curly-haired girl from his class was on the ground. Her forehead was bleeding. An ache burst in Julian's stomach. He took a step forward. Quinn nudged him back into position. The tall guy picked her up and ran towards the Hilton. Thank you, Julian said to himself.

Just as he lost sight of them, the cops started smashing the windows of a restaurant in the Hilton. Four or five of them jumped through the broken window. Their anger was palpable even at a distance. Julian wished he were dreaming. He hadn't signed up for a war. Just for the games.

"Julian!" he heard someone scream. "Julian!"

Kari was staggering towards him, holding her shoulder, wincing in pain. Tears were streaming down her face. Tear gas.

197

What the hell? His own eyes began to burn. "Kari!" he yelled, without thinking. Quinn brought his rifle down hard on Julian's boot. Julian kicked it away. He started moving out of line. Quinn raised his rifle and held it sideways in front of Julian. Julian stepped back. Then a cop headed right for Kari. Julian saw the fear in her eyes.

The blood rushed to Julian's face, making him dizzy. He swayed in place for a moment; then he pushed Quinn's rifle aside and ran at the cop.

"Michaels! Get your ass back here," McCoy shouted.

Julian shoved a cop, who turned on him, eyes squinting, mouth drawn down into an inverted "U," billy club raised, ready to pummel him.

"That's my sister!"

"Get back to the curb, you fucking asshole," the cop shouted, his billy club still dangling in the air.

"Leave her alone," Julian screamed. He pointed his rifle at the cop.

"Get out of my way, or I'll break your fucking head."

Kari ducked around the cop. Julian watched her race towards the relative safety of the hotel. Still, he stood his ground for a long moment. Then he cocked his head, lowered his gun, smiled at the cop, and walked slowly back to his position.

The sound of Alex's laughter chuckled in his brain. "See ya later alligator," Alex whispered, as he drifted permanently out of sight.

"After while crocodile," Julian said to no one in particular.

Chapter Fifteen

Home

Mike wasn't sure how long he'd been walking. Then running. Hours probably. It felt more like days. Months. Years. All his life. He'd automatically headed in the direction of Bridgeport. Headed home. He could feel the stares. He didn't care. Didn't care about anything anymore. In one moment of fear and rage, he'd somehow become his worst enemy.

He was glad it was dark by the time he reached his house. He didn't want his neighbors to see his shame. He threw back his sinking shoulders, and with a last shot of adrenalin, unlocked the front door and walked into the little hallway. If only I'd stayed in bed this morning, like I wanted to, he thought. Not with anger. But with sadness. The kind of sadness you have when you've lost something and know it's gone forever. Even if it's something you don't care about, really. Or don't even like or want.

Maureen stood at the top of the stairs, obviously startled by the noise. He could hear the boys upstairs. Fighting in the bathroom before bedtime, as usual.

"Mike?"

"Yeah."

"Been watching the news. Didn't expect you home so early."

I told you not to let the kids watch the news, he wanted to scream at her. What if they'd seen him like that? "I'm home," was the only thing he said. At the same time, he wasn't sure exactly what that meant. He didn't feel like he was home. Nothing felt familiar.

"You okay?"

He didn't know how to answer that. Was he okay? Would he ever be okay again? "No," he said, finally.

Maureen walked down one step. She eyed him up and down. One of the boys yelled, "Mom, tell him to stop." Another one yelled, "Shut up, crybaby."

"The kids. Let me just take care of . . ."

"I'm okay."

Maureen turned and walked back up the step. He could hear her in the bathroom, not exactly yelling at the kids. More like giving them directions in a no-nonsense tone of voice. Kind of the way she talked to him, he thought. It seemed to work.

He walked into the kitchen. She'd already cleared the dinner table and done the dishes. Dinner for him would be in the refrigerator. He'd just need to warm it up. It would be corn beef and cabbage or a piece of red meat. Potatoes. The same kind of food his mother made when he was a kid. Still made. The thought of it turned his stomach. He'd seen enough raw flesh that day. He grabbed a glass from the cupboard and filled it with water; then drank it down in one long gulp. Filled it again and drank that down, too. For a moment he thought about pouring it over his head to cool down his brain.

He looked out the open kitchen window into the night. There was just enough light from the bulb over the kitchen sink to watch leaves on the trees in the back yard move silently in the breeze. Wave at him. As if they knew. He could hear sprinkles of laughter and wondered if he'd ever laugh again. He heard Frances O'Donnell from next door yell at her kids to come in. I went to grade school with Frances, he thought. One time she'd told him that he wasn't anything like his brothers. He'd blanched, thinking she'd meant he wasn't as tough or popular or maybe smart, though he knew he was smarter than they were. But that's not what she'd meant, at all. "They're mean," she said. Then she blushed and said, "But I can't tell you why." And she ran off.

Maybe I should ask her some day. Why she thought my brothers were mean. They were mean. Like the old man. Liked to fight. Get into trouble with the Farrell boys down the street. Should have been a priest like my mother said. Oh yeah. Right. It was bad enough being an alter boy. Mike shivered. That's when I started dreaming about him—the fuckin' man with the green measles, he thought suddenly. That first year I was an alter boy. And every year after.

Mike began slowly unbuttoning his shirt. Then he ripped it off. He leaned against the wall and took off his shoes and socks, undid his belt, unzipped his pants and let them drop to the floor. He stepped out of his jockey shorts and kicked his clothes to the side.

Maureen walked into the kitchen. "For Christ's sake, Mike. What are you doing?"

He kept staring out the window.

"Mike!"

"Yeah."

"What if the kids walk in?"

"What if they do?" he growled at her, surprising himself by the tone of his voice which actually seemed be someone else's voice coming out of his mouth. Or, at least, from out of someone else's gut.

He could hear by the intake of her breath that he'd surprised Maureen, too. He smiled to himself.

"Mike," she said more softly. "What happened?"

"I swallowed a beast."

"I don't understand."

"Me neither." He turned around and looked at her. She was twenty pounds overweight, but she was still a beautiful woman in some ways. And he loved her and boys. I just don't know who they are, he thought. Don't know who I am.

"I'll get your bathrobe." She turned to leave the room.

He knew she was anxious to get away from him. He wasn't himself. And she didn't know who he was. I'm a stranger in my own house, he thought. Taking up too much space.

"No," he said, not unkindly. "I don't want my bathrobe."

She turned back to look at him again. Quizzically. As if she hadn't heard him correctly. She tilted her head to the side and blinked. "Okay," she said, finally. Then she walked slowly out of the room.

Mike watched her disappear into the shadows. And for a moment, he thought about calling out to her. Instead, he pivoted around to look out of the window again. He knew instinctively that the man with the green measles would never chase him again. He'd beaten him back. He was relieved. At the same time, he recognized that his actions in the park made him no different from his brothers. Or his father. Or the man with the green measles, for that matter. And he was profoundly shaken.

Chapter Sixteen

Dividends

Helen expects her life to flash in front of her. But that's not the way it's happening. Why should it, she thinks. Nothing in my life turned out to be as I expected. Why should my death?

She has no illusions that Godot will rescue her at the last moment. Or that the deus ex machina will descend. But she sees. And more important, feels the story of her life as it presents itself. Not in a flash. But slowly. Bit by bit.

She reaches for Octavia's hand, willing her to witness what she could never allow herself to reveal.

"Trust no one," she hears Franz whisper. She looks across the border dividing Austria from Czechoslovakia and knows in the pit of her stomach that she will never see him again. "Go," he says fiercely. He shoves her towards the checkpoint. Without looking back, she walks slowly towards freedom, her false identification papers in her pocket, her mother's diamond engagement ring and diamond necklace in the lining of her coat, the money she will need inside her undergarments, scratching at her, reminding her with every step that her life will never be the same once she crosses the divide.

I am afraid, she thinks. The fear rises to my throat. I choke on it. The chomp of dried leaves under my feet echoes my fear.

It's the end of March. The ground still hoards the crunch of winter. The sound of my footsteps fills the silence, growing louder and louder like the sound of Hitler's planes when they circled Vienna. I tremble. I see Von Schuschnigg's words in the patterns of the leaves and know that he will do nothing to protect us. I expect the soldier guarding the border to point his gun at me. For a moment, I hope he shoots me dead. Then my journey will be over; there will be nothing more to fear.

She hears the whispers of her family and their friends. In her imagination, they march along beside her, egging her on. "Schuschnigg has sold Austria's soul to the devil," Zweig says. No one believes him except my brother and my grandmother, whose face is my face—who was also 18 when she crossed the Austrian border. Now I hold her passport that my brother has altered, so I can cross back into Czechoslovakia—into safety—just in case.

A sudden surge of anger tackles my fear. Just in case? The walls are crashing down. And still they talk about "Handsome" Karl Leuger who rode into power on his anti-Semitic platform. I have to tell Octavia, Helen thinks. Do you hear me, Octavia? "We will survive," my father says. "We aren't religious. We are as Viennese as our Catholic neighbors." Yes, yes. I try to convince myself as I finger the passport in my pocket. My father is a doctor, my mother an opera singer, Franz is at the University. They will be safe. And yet—and yet—I am crossing the border into another life.

I feel pain, unbearable pain, shoot through my body, and I think the soldier has smacked me with the butt of his rifle; then I remember where I am. I don't open my eyes.

I want to find myself.

Was it then, I wonder. Was it when they searched my body at each border that I began to forget? Was it in the over-crowded, unsanitary trains, one body melting into another, so we—I—had no choice but to lose myself? The trains, the trains, the trains, she thinks. Sweltering and horrible. But not deathly. Not yet. We don't know yet that there will be other trains from which there will be no escape. Still, only the persistent clanging of the wheels drives out the groans, the smells of sweating bodies and vanishing hope. It is easier to get lost in the sound of the wheels than to hear the sounds of voices still clinging to a language that she can not listen to. Even now. The musical accent of Viennese German is a lie; a mask. "Achtung" means the same thing no matter how you say it, she thinks. I hear it spoken at every checkpoint, in every train I take. The transit visas I manage to procure, like some convict hunted by the police, lead me in the opposite direction, away from them, away from my home.

My body itches. I try to scratch, but I can't raise my hand from this bed in a stranger's house. Someone touches me. I think it's my grandmother. She speaks to me in Czech, sometimes in Yiddish. I answer her with the few words I know. We speak High German in our house. Sometimes French. English with the nanny. No Yiddish, except when my father jokes with Dr. Freud. Can it be my grandmother? Am I in her bed?

I am confused. I disgorge from the train that has chugged its way from Prague to Nice. I make my way around the unoccupied city. But I am still afraid to breathe. Where can I change my money? I hear people speaking German and know they are Jews. I don't approach them. I see the sign in front of a small pension tucked into a winding street: "Room for rent." I knock softly. The woman who owns the pension comes to the door. She is even thinner than I am and much older. I look into her eyes; then shift my gaze to her scant hair dyed a rusty color. She waits for me to speak. Finally, I tell her that I am a student. She doesn't ask for my passport; I don't offer it. I still don't look at her, afraid she will guess my secret, afraid she's already guessed it. For the first time in my life, I feel humiliated.

I sit on the hard wooden floor of my tiny room and count the faded flowers on the wallpaper. I promise myself that I will stop counting when I finish the wall opposite me. But I can't. I will count everything—the number of houses on a street, the number of letters in a sign, the number of people standing on the corner—until I can move on to my final destination—where I'm headed now. Too soon and too late.

I wait for my visa. Four million other refugees trapped in southern France also wait for theirs. I study English so I can perfect the language I learned from my English nanny. I will never speak German again. Never.

The smell of steaming croissants lingers. And for a moment I am ravenous. There is never enough to eat. Only collaborators are fat.

Varian Fry tells me that there are no visas. Only for people with exceptional merit. President Roosevelt's committee has to approve, etc. etc. etc. The blood boils up inside of me. I stand there staring into his eyes. He blinks. If I ever get to America, I will become a person of exceptional merit, I think. Then I think if I get to America, I will not need to become a person of exceptional merit.

That is the first death. There were many others.

"Does she hear me?"

"It's hard to tell. She's refused to take her medication. Wanted to be alert; she knew you were coming."

Helen searches her mind. Who are they talking about, she wonders. Who are they? Someone touches my hand again. I try to move it away. I do not like to be touched by strangers. But the touch is somehow familiar.

"Mother . . ."

Whose mother does she speak to? Is she filled with loneliness and sorrow?

I hum "Liebestod" under my breath as my mother sings Isolde's final aria. I cannot bear to watch her die upon Tristan's body. I cannot bear to look away.

I will not listen to Wagner again. I ask my uncle not to play it. I ask him how he found me, how he was able to get the visa for me. He's vague at first; then says that his friend is a United States senator. I wonder why he couldn't help his brother—who is my father, and my mother, my brother and my grandmother—his mother. But I don't ask. I am shy. I am stunned. I feel. And I don't feel. Then I remember that I must become a person of exceptional merit—just in case.

Uncle Stefan Landsman has become Stephen Lang. I take his last name. I keep my grandmother's first name, the name on her passport—now my passport. My good luck piece.

But I am in a stranger's bed now. I use all of my strength to raise my eyelids. I see my grandmother's eyes, black like mine. My heart melts as she touches my face. I am a little girl again. And for a moment, the pain is gone.

I can't keep my eyes open any longer, Helen thinks. But just as she closes them, she sees the white blond hair. My grandmother's hair was dark, like mine. I see the thick black eyebrows and the white hair. And suddenly, I remember. It is my daughter who holds my hand.

I try to tell Octavia to find the key to my locked cabinet and take out the passport. I want to hold it. But I'm not sure I can find the right words.

The locked cabinet, the story of my other life, will be her legacy. She will find what is left of my family, of our house, the photographs, the pictures of Vienna cut from magazines. Of Vienna before and after the war. Not the city it used to be—and never was. It was all an illusion: gorgeous ornate buildings, pastries and coffee mit schlag at Demel's, music floating from the Danube to the Hothe Warte. An intoxicating city with a putrid soul. Rotting from the beginning. People parading around the Ringstrasse in their finest, stopping at St. Stephan's to cleanse their sins so they would be free to sin again. And how was it a sin, they must have thought, when the Cardinal rang the bells to welcome Hitler? The savior has come to oust the renegade Jews.

I hear them now—the bells of St. Stephan's. I cross the Ringstrasse to the Opera to meet my mother. As I walk through the ornate lobby, I pretend to be a princess, the tragic heroine of my dying kingdom. In her dressing room, she still wears her stage makeup, her wig, and her costume. I feel shy in front of her beauty which both transcends reality and is totally real to me. She has sung Traviata, my favorite. I reach out to her. But she disappears.

"We must get you new clothes." This is the first thing my uncle says to me as I get off the train.

I have not seen him since I was a little girl. I don't remember him at all. His letters, with their news of America, stopped coming years ago.

"How did you recognize me?"

"By your clothes."

"I have other clothes in my suitcase."

"Thank God your English is commendable. Just as your brother promised. Come quickly," he says, as if he doesn't want anyone to see me. "You look like a foreigner. My wife will take you shopping tomorrow."

"Thank you for your generosity, Uncle Stefan."

"Stephen. Stephen Lang. Mercedes doesn't know me by Stefan. Or Landsman. Please don't refer to me in that way."

"Mercedes is your wife, then?"

"Yes. And you are my niece from England."

I understand. I smile at the deception. And why not?

"Goethe Street?" I say as we pull up in front of a brownstone building. I am shocked that the Americans would name a street after a German writer.

My uncle smiles for the first time. "Go thee," he says. The Americans don't say Goethe."

"Go thee?"

"You'll get used to it."

He smiles at me again. And I breathe. He will not be a villain who takes in his impoverished niece and mistreats her, as the villains do in the novels by Dickens I have read.

By day I am Helen Lang. I sit in my art history class at the University of Chicago and study fifteenth century triptychs. I pour over pages from illuminated manuscripts. In my imagination, I lightly trace the elongated white faces of Saint Peter and the cerulean gowns trimmed in gold leaf, worn by Mother Mary. I touch the blood spurting out from the crown of thorns. With a magnifying glass, I study the perfectly painted minute figures in the background and along the edges of the page. I wonder how heathens could have evolved from such an elegant people.

"Stop," I say out loud. Or maybe not. Maybe I just think it. No more about the war. I try not to think about it. I gasp. I am choking. I feel her hands gently picking me up. I stop choking. She helps me to lie down again. I open my eyes and see the television across the room. I want to turn my head away. But I see that people are afraid. They're running. My God, they are running here—in Chicago. It's not a movie. I see the Band Shell in Grant Park, where we attend concerts in summer. Is it summer? The Nazis are hunting them down, smashing people's heads. I try to grab my daughter's hand to ask her if they are hunting down the Jews. If this is happening in America. Hide. Quickly. Before the Gestapo knocks down the door. The train out of Nice to Drancy. Don't step aboard. If I had gone to Drancy—If I hadn't run—

I am sweating from every pore in my body. What does it matter that I live in an elegant brownstone on Goethe Street and that I wear American clothes which Mercedes has chosen for me. They will find the key. They will open my cabinet. And they will know. I knew Christians in Vienna; friends from school. My father's patients were Christians. Did he knock on their doors at the end? Did they turn him away?

Mercedes and Uncle Stephen aren't Catholic; they are Episcopalian. They tell me it's like Anglicans. Not so different from the Catholic church, but they don't follow the dictates of the pope. I'm glad they're not Catholic. I remember the Cardinal's embrace of Hitler.

I sit stiffly on the wooden bench and feel the hard surface under my thighs. My soft white kidskin gloves sit primly in my lap. I am dressed like an American in a sleek grey linen suit with a short jacket and a white blouse with a Peter Pan collar. I read the prayer book and am fascinated by the stories from the New Testament, the Christian Bible. But when we pray together, I keep my lips sealed and refuse to say "our Lord Jesus Christ" or "in the name of the Father, the Son, and the Holy Ghost." I look like an American. But I feel as if I have been misplaced. Or I have somehow misplaced myself. I have to recreate myself from scratch, like the Golem, molded out of clay. Only I couldn't save the Jews from destruction. Did the Golem feel? Do I? I think not. I am somehow beyond feeling. I hear the choir singing "Onward Christian Soldiers marching off to war with the cross of Jesus . . ." It keeps spinning through my head. Were they singing that when they marched up Bergasse? As I sit there in church, I promise myself that once I leave my uncle's house, I will become a Jew again. A Jew who is exceptional. Even in America it might be necessary.

I try to get out of my body, which is filled with poison. Knives stab at my stomach. At my breast. They hurt less than the knives that stab my soul. I must remember who I am—or who I was. But I'm afraid that I have forgotten too much. I see my mother's face. But it is hidden behind stage makeup. She is Violetta till the end of her days. As I am. We both play our parts. I look at my daughter hoping to find my mother's face in hers. But it's just the eyes. The face is her father's. And he's a stranger to me. As I am to him.

I sit in the beauty parlor with Mercedes. Snippets of my black hair whirl around the tile floor. I look at myself in the mirror. I'm transformed. The braids that I wound around my head are gone. My hair is combed under into a page boy. I begin to look like Mercedes. My thick eyebrows are plucked thin, ruby lipstick is applied to my lips, and I hear Mercedes—she insists that I call her Mercedes and not aunt—say that I look like Snow White with my black hair, white skin, and ruby lips. "Some day soon your prince will come," she says light-heartedly. My back stiffens. I want to cry. But I don't. Never. Not even when my uncle holds the letter in his hands and cries. We talk of war but never mention history.

The shouting on the television slices through me. I see them in newsreels in the theater. The ones who survived. If you can call it that. I sit through the movies, once, twice, three times just to see the newsreels again and again, but I never find them.

I stand at the door of Dr. Freud's little house in England. I want to call out to Anna, tell her I've come to collect my history. I raise my hand to the knocker and let it slowly hit the door; then I run as fast as I can.

We sit at a table for twelve in my uncle's spacious apartment. China and crystal glitter. The maid has polished the silver. A Christmas tree stands in the living room. There is no cross on top of it, though it annoys Mercedes that my uncle won't let her adorn the tree with her family heirloom. We, too, had a Christmas tree in Vienna. All the Jews did. All of us who were assimilated. It represented the winter solstice, we told ourselves. I assiduously avoid saying the word "Christ," even to myself. No matter that I sit in church with my aunt and my uncle. My uncle who was my savior. Jesus is not.

"Helen," she hears her uncle say. But he isn't talking to her. He's talking to a tall, handsome man with white blond hair and deep blue eyes. He's younger than her uncle. Well, she thinks, with his Aryan looks he would have easily escaped. Then she laughs to herself. He is obviously not a Jew. "Helen has come to live with us because it's too dangerous in London. We were thrilled when her brother contacted us."

"Where is your family now?" the blond-haired man asks. Somehow she hadn't caught his name. But his question hangs in the air. She doesn't answer.

"I hope they're safe," he says earnestly.

"Yes," she says finally.

Her uncle changes the subject. They talk about the snow blanketing the city and the difficulty of getting around. And she thinks that once the Germans came, everything ran on time. They shaped up the Austrians, didn't they? Those café-loving Jews disappeared into the wilderness, leaving Vienna without anyone to play the Strauss waltzes.

She hears herself moaning and squeezes her eyes shut for a moment; then she hears a man's voice from across the room. She opens her eyes. The man is on television. He stands at a podium and raises his hand. She's afraid he will say, "Heil Hitler." Instead he seems angry about the Gestapo. The Gestapo is everywhere, she thinks. People are bleeding and screaming. Crying for help. Surely, they will arrest the man on the podium; then deport him.

In my locked cabinet which I bequeath to my daughter are photographs of Mauthausen, where my parents were sent to retire. It's a lovely little country town with rolling hills. When I look at the Super 8 film of my friend Josephine's trip to Austria many years after my parents are dead, I notice the McDonald's at the foot of the winding road up to the camp. "Arbeit macht frei," I say. Then I change the last word to English and laugh at the gallows humor. "Work makes you free—or in this case, fries," I whisper.

"I didn't know you spoke German," Josephine says.

"I don't," I answer.

I look at the photograph of the children's bunkhouse with rows of little wooden bunk beds, like summer camp. I do not allow my daughter to buy bunk beds. When we go to the furniture store, and she climbs up on them, the bones in my knees begin to disintegrate. I am afraid that I will float to the ground in a sigh of despair. The wood is highly polished. The Germans always did everything beautifully. Out of the window, I notice cows roaming nearby. I can make out a barbed wire fence separating them from the grounds of the camp.

I look away from the film and try to breathe normally. But I am afraid that my heart will pound so loudly that Josephine will hear it. I remember my trick and place my feet solidly on the floor. I think of clarinets playing over the strings. I hear my mother singing Fiordiligi's aria from the first act of Così Fan Tutte. I concentrate with all of my might, my fingernails buried deep in the palms of my hands.

I try not to look. But out of the corner of my eye, I see the stone quarry. I count the steps as my friend walks down them. Over a hundred. I see my parents lugging stones up and down the steps, dozens of them every day until they drop.

I should have walked those steps with their ghosts.

As I lie here in this stranger's bed, I ask myself who I am. I can't answer that question.

The man with the white-blond hair looks deeply into my eyes and says that he has never met anyone like me. I laugh. But I know that it's true. When he makes love to me, the noises in my brain shift. I take him into me, then release him like the sweet sounds of a trumpet. Not the sad notes announcing Mahler's Fifth; the bitter-sweet sound of Louis Armstrong.

The man with white-blond hair is perfect. But I am broken. Still, I am my mother's daughter. On our twentieth anniversary, he gives me a diamond necklace. It is elegant and expensive. He would like to put it around my neck. But I evade him. Still, he smiles and hums to himself as he dresses for dinner. For the first time, I notice the slump of his shoulders. And I am afraid—then relieved. Finally, a feeling comes over me that surely mimics love.

I run my hand down Octavia's silky hair. All these years, and I never quite believed that I am the mother of this perfect Aryan child. She is not brilliant; she is not musical; she is not exceptional. She doesn't have to be. Her laughter is more pure than Beethoven's greatest symphony. I hear her in my soul. And I begin to wake up. Her tiny fingers touch my lips, and I expel words of love. I learn to laugh again. I almost convince myself that I am alive.

I wanted to re-write history. But history has come back to haunt me.

I feel Octavia's cool hand on my face. I must look at her, hold her close before she floats into another world. Before I fade away. "Octavia," I whisper. "Remember."

My grandmother's hands tell me she loves me. I reach out to her. They cannot murder love. *"Ich bin a Yid,"* I say clearly.

Chapter Seventeen

The Beginning

On her birth day, she is an orphan. Aware and unaware. Swimming in the waters of Babylon, she carries the seed of creation that transcends time and space. She is a tiny speck drifting in the vast collective unconscious. She knows who she was. Who she is. Who she will be. In the last delicious moment before her birth, she is herself; and she is everyone.

She lies under a huge weeping willow tree, her back pressed against the fresh grass. It feels cool under her navy blue pinafore. She barely notices the red and yellow roses working their way up the U-shaped trellis across from her. Instead, she stares at the sky. Leaves of the willow tree blow in the wind. She feels the wind on her bare arms and legs. She feels it brush her face. White clouds drift by; each one is a different shape. There's a horse. There's a whale. There's a lion. There's a man with a beard. They go by before I get a chance to know them. Fast. Faster. I'll go into the house as soon as I count three more animals. The shapes I see are people or animals that have died. I count five more. Still I lie here. What if my mother floats by and I miss her? She holds a woman's hand. They walk up the steep hill. The woman is and is not my mother, she thinks. She's old. I'm embarrassed. She's taught me to hold my head high. She's taught me to be strong. She's taught me that love conquers sorrow. Which I feel even before I understand what either love or sorrow is. She's the only mother I have ever known. But not the only mother I will know.

She sees that I'm about to cry and squeezes my hand tightly. "I remember your mama's first morning at Country Day," she says. "Your grandma, she brought her here. Like I'm bringin' you. Then your grandma came home and cried all the day long, until it was time to pick your mama up. You look just like your mama, you know, except for your dark hair. You have her black eyes. Black eyes like your grandma's, too. And your grandma's black hair."

"My daddy had dark hair. In the picture."

"Yes, he did."

"Did you take care of him, too?"

"I only met your daddy one time, honey."

We walk towards one of the buildings on the grounds of the school. I'm afraid that everyone will stare at us because we look different. I feel love for this wrinkled old black woman who embarrasses me. But I also feel shame.

There are big kids tossing balls on the huge lawn between the buildings. They fly across the lawn and knock into each other and laugh. I'm too little. They won't see me. They'll knock me down. I want to hide behind Millie's skirt.

"Your mama was never scared again—after that first day. She was never afraid of anything again," Millie says.

But she should have been, the little girl thinks. And it doesn't make her feel better. It makes her feel worse. She is afraid of everything.

She looks through the window into her classroom. She sees a long-faced woman with short blond hair. The woman wears a blue skirt and a matching blouse. I'm already afraid of her. I'm different from the other children. Opa says not to say kids. All the other children do. I say children. They all say grandpa. I say

217

Opa. I don't want Opa to be angry with me. Will the teacher like me? Will she think Millie's my mother? What if she thinks Millie's my mother? I feel sick to my stomach. We make too much noise when we open the door. But she smiles at me when we walk into the room. That's all I see at first. Her smile. She has big teeth. The better to eat me with? I feel shy and look around the room filled with low desks and colorful posters. She takes my hand and squats down in front of me. She takes me in.

The little girl sits at a desk and colors. The girl next to her has a silver crayon. She yearns for it with a kind of yearning she doesn't really understand yet. I could ask Opa to buy me one. But I won't do that. I made a rule not to ask him for anything. I think he gives Millie lots of dollars to buy me what I need. Sometimes she buys me things I don't need. That's the most fun. But not enough fun to fill her up. There's a bucket inside of her. Millie tries to fill it with hugs and kisses. With cookies and milk. With sweet words. But there's a little hole at the bottom of the bucket.

At recess everyone goes outside. She stays in the room. She looks at the silver crayon. She picks it up and smells it. She makes a star on her paper and colors it in with the silver crayon. She draws a moon. Not a full moon. Just a sliver. Her teacher smiles at her. "I'll walk outside with you," she says, "to play with the other children." She turns her paper over and slips the silver crayon into her pocket.

When they go outside, the girl who owns the silver crayon asks her if she wants to jump rope. She nods. They jump rope until it's time to go inside again.

"Where's my silver crayon?" the other girl asks. She looks through all the crayons on her desk. She turns the crayon box upside down and shakes it.

"Oh," she says, "I found it on the floor." She takes it out of her pocket and hands it to the girl.

"Thank you," the girl says politely. Then she hands it back. "You can use it if you want to."

Marcia, the owner of silver crayon, stands next to her at her Communion. She searches the stories in the stained glass windows of the church looking for clues. She sees Opa sitting at the back of the church with Millie. He looks tired. Suddenly she feels frightened. What if he dies, she thinks.

There are 13 candles on her cake. Marcia and eight other girls from her class sit at the dining room table. They squeal when she opens each present. She's polite. Millie has taught her to be polite. She thanks each of them. It's almost May. But the weather hasn't changed yet. They all wear linen dresses with long sleeves.

Peter and Becky are here too. Peter's tall. Becky's short and a little chubby. Not a lot. She jokes about it. She's wearing black slacks and a green silk blouse, my favorite blouse, in honor of my birthday. I like the way she looks. She baked my birthday cake. My grandfather avoids speaking to her. She doesn't care. I got my period yesterday. I'm embarrassed to look at Opa. I hunch my shoulders to hide my breasts. I could talk to Millie if she were here. But maybe not. She was so old.

Opa's gift to me is a key. Automatically, I get up from the table and walk into the library. I know what the key is for. I walk straight to the cabinet, which is always locked. I stand there, afraid to open it; afraid not to.

Becky stands behind me. She puts her hand on my shoulder. I jump. "Sorry," she says. "Why don't you open it later? Your friends are all waiting for you."

I feel my mother's sorrow. Inside her body, I kick three times to let her know that I know. I know everything she thinks and feels, but I also know that I won't remember later. I know that on August 28, 1968 my grandmother Helen was dying. I know that many innocent people, in a country I will never visit, also died that day. And that's why I didn't. I see the motorcycle racing down the street. I see my father's long hair flying in the wind. I see him swerve to miss a rickshaw and slam into an armored tank. I hear people screaming. I see Peter standing next to my mother at the cemetery. I see her big belly as she leans against him.

I sit with Opa on a hard bench at the back of the small church with a scarred wooden floor. There is nothing elegant about the church. But the room reverberates with feeling. Everyone is crying. Singing and crying. "Praise Jesus; Praise the Lord," they say over and over again. The service is long. Many people walk up to the pulpit to speak. The women all wear fancy hats. I squirm. But I don't want to leave. I stare at the one stained glass window in the room. It tells the story of the resurrection, and suddenly I wonder if it was really true or if it's just a story.

"Our sister Millie Washington was a woman of God," the minister says. Millie called him her preacher. "Praise the Lord," the congregation answers. "Sing Halleluiah," he says. The choir sways back and forth and starts singing as if they really mean it. What if God is just a story?

"Gee zus," someone calls out.

"Lord. Lord," someone else answers.

She cranes her neck to see where it's coming from.

People are singing and clapping. She drifts off.

"Your mama had blond hair, almost white," Millie says, as she combs out my hair. "Your hair is black, just like your grandmother's. Your mama was the most beautiful little girl."

I look at myself in the mirror and think that I am not beautiful. Or Millie would have said so.

I'm uncomfortable. I don't belong here. This is exactly where I belong.

I don't belong anywhere.

I see flowers. Many flowers wrapped around a trellis. A man in a long black robe faces Peter who stands under the trellis, next to Becky. He's crying. So is Becky. She laughs at her tears. A dour-looking old woman with big sagging breasts and a smiling old man, who's also crying, stand behind her. For a moment, I don't know who they are. Then I understand that they're Becky's parents. They look nothing like Peter's parents who stand stiffly behind him: elegant, uncomfortable. Peter smashes a glass with his foot. Almost everyone cheers.

Becky walks into the library with her and closes the door. She hands Helen the key. She opens her grandmother's cabinet. "Did my mother ever open it?" she asks Becky.

"I don't know."

She looks at her. "Has Opa ever opened it?"

"Opa told Peter that your grandmother gave your mother the key just before she died. And then—and then . . ."

"My father died. And then she did. From an allergic reaction to the anesthesia." She doesn't know exactly what that means. Only that one minute her mother was alive. And the next she wasn't. "Did you know him?"

"No. But it feels like I did. He was Peter's best friend. And after your father died, he and your mother helped each other. You know—tried to focus on you."

"Millie told me. He was there when I was born. Opa's going to die."

"Yes."

"Soon."

"I don't know."

"Then I'll be more than an orphan. Millie's gone, too," she says. What she can't say is that she's terrified. Who will take care of me, she wonders.

"We've talked about it. Peter and I love you, Helen."

Helen hears her. But from a distance. As if she doesn't quite own her name. Opa still calls her little Helen.

"Didn't you go to school with them?" Helen asks suddenly.

Becky laughs. "Not exactly."

She sounds strange when she says words like "not," Helen thinks. It sounds more like "nat." Becky's father talks the same way. Opa says they're uneducated. But that's not exactly what he means.

"Do you want me to stay with you?"

"Yes, please stay."

Her hand shakes; she can't get the key into the lock. She's embarrassed. Becky puts her hand on Helen's arm. Helen doesn't look at her. But she sees her. Becky has the same dark curly hair that my grandmother had. That I have. But her eyes are green. Cat's eyes, Peter says.

She unlocks the cabinet and takes out a large box. They put the box on the long glass-topped library table that runs down the middle of the room. She's afraid to open it. She looks at Becky. Then takes off the lid. There are a pile of papers inside. She picks up an old passport. It's from 1920. She doesn't recognize the last name. But the first name is "Helen."

Becky frowns.

"Czechoslovakia. That's weird."

"May I see it?"

Helen hands the passport to her.

"Helen Landsman," Becky says. "Was your grandmother from Czechoslovakia?"

"From England. And her name was Lang. This must have belonged to another Helen."

Helen watches her study the passport; then she follows Becky's eyes to a large black and white photograph of her grandmother Helen, which sits on top of the cabinet.

Helen notes the photograph, too. Her grandmother looks young. For a moment, it seems strange that her grandmother looks about the same age as she is now. She also died before I was born. It makes her sad, and she turns away from the photo. But the seed inside of me, inside of my mother, expands to travel time, she thinks. I am the Helen who will be. And at the same time, I am also the Helen who was.

Becky hands the passport back to me. She analyzes my face as if she's looking for clues to something. I see Austria, Czechoslovakia, France, and England stamped in the passport. The last stamp is the United States.

I move aside a pile of papers and find some old photographs. I turn one over then hand it to Becky. She reads the German; then translates: "Papa, Mama, Franz and me in front of the Opera. 1935." She returns the photo. I stare at the four people. I look at the photo of my grandmother on the cabinet and look at the photo I'm holding. I glance at Becky. She's lost in an old yellowed newspaper article. I pick up another photo of a woman in a costume and heavy makeup. I turn that one over. I can figure out what it says without Becky's help. "Mama as Violetta. 1936."

I rifle through the papers: other old newspapers, letters from Vienna written in German. I pick up a file with some kind of report. At the end of the report it says in English:

"Otto Landsman, deceased, Auschwitz December 15, 1942.

Hanna Landsman, deceased Auschwitz, May 22, 1943.

Helen Landsman, deceased Auschwitz, August 1, 1944.

Franz Landsman, whereabouts unknown.

I know what Auschwitz is. I'm confused. My grandmother's name was Helen. My name is Helen. Who is this other Helen? And why is she in my grandmother's secret cabinet? I notice that this Helen was the last to die.

Becky is now staring at me. She looks like she's about to cry. Becky puts her arms around me. We both start to cry.

"Does Opa know?"

"I don't think so."

The air's especially oppressive in the Old City. Finally, they make their way to the Mount of Olives. Helen hears the call of the muezzin in the background. In what sounds like a competition, Hebrew prayers from the Wailing Wall reach a high pitch. I'm a stranger here, Helen thinks. And I'm not a stranger. I carry my grandmother's history.

"Plot 16, row 35," Peter says as they keep their eyes to the ground, searching each tombstone.

"Franz Landsman," Becky says. "1919-1955."

Helen watches Becky put a small stone on his grave. She picks up a stone and does the same. "Can you say a prayer?"

"No," Becky answers. "But I know them."

"Teach me."

Becky looks at Helen for a long time. "It's mythology."

"It's also history."

Helen, Becky and Peter walk the Via Dolorosa, crammed with noisy tourists. They're shocked to find the Stations of the Cross so close together. Inside the Church of Notre Dame de Zion, they look down on the original brick-paved street that Jesus walked. This is history, Helen thinks. It's a part of my history. Just as the Wailing Wall is a part of my history. I want to suck up history and keep it alive inside of me.

I am me—Helen—the Helen now inside of my mother's body, the Helen who was my grandmother, whose genes reside in me. I am Helen of Troy. I am all the Helens who have created our own histories. We tell ourselves stories in order to remember who we were and who we are.

Becky comes rushing up. In the sunlight, Helen notices the grey in her curly hair, the wrinkles around her mouth. Out of breath, she explains that she's working with a journalism professor from Northwestern and some of his students. They think they've discovered evidence that would free a man on death row. "Firm hates it when I take too many pro bono cases. But this one's too important to pass up."

"They're all too important to pass up."

"Interesting guy. The professor. Irish. He was a cop during the sixties. Quit after the demonstration in Grant Park. Probably the cop who busted my head."

She laughs and points to the stitches in her forehead. Only a faint scar remains. "Not really. He had black eyes, not blue." Helen smiles at Becky. And a moment later her colleague Harvey Bender and his wife Suzanne, who's older than Becky but still looks like a girl, rush over to greet them. They reminisce about another time they were here. This crowd is tame. The cops mill around in the background. There's anger but not menace.

Peter puts his arm around Becky and says to Helen's husband Rob, "Did Becky ever tell you this is where we met?

Helen's father was here, too. He covered the demonstration for the 'Sun-Times'; she was still a blip inside of Octavia."

"It was the longest courtship in history," Helen says, jokingly.

Then she lurches backward to before the beginning of her time. All her tiny limbs are in motion at once—as if she's trying to fight and conquer Fate. At the same time, the self outside her mother's body, the self-standing with Becky and Peter, her husband Rob, and the Benders feels what the fetus feels. And for that moment, knows what the fetus knows. The mention of my mother's name still leaves me with a residue of sadness, she thinks. She acknowledges the sadness. Then tucks it away to visit at another time. Even after she's born, this will always remain with her. Long after all the other memories have faded, this sadness has somehow been encoded into her DNA. A personal sadness and a collective sadness.

"He rescued me when an overzealous policeman smashed my head with his billy club. But we didn't meet again for another ten years."

"Quite by accident."

"Not exactly."

Helen smiles. She knows there are no accidents.

The baby begins her journey through the passage of time to the other side of knowledge. She wonders if there's a way to keep her Self in tact. And knows there will be only glimpses. Perhaps the glimpses will be enough, she thinks. I feel a tug, a push, a shove, hands on my head pulling me down. For a moment, I resist. I cling to my mother because I know. I weep with a longing that will never quite go away. I know I will not see her. Will not know her. And yet. And yet—I do.

About Marilyn Levy

Marilyn Levy was born in Youngstown, Ohio, and has lived most of her life in the Chicago area and in Los Angeles. Trained initially as a teacher, Levy has also worked as a writer in the film industry; she has written and published eighteen books; and she maintains a private counseling practice in Santa Monica, California. Her novels have been recognized for excellence by the American Library Association Best Book List, the New York Public Library Best Book List, the Society of School Librarians International Best Book Award, and the Jewish Publication Society. Levy's work as a film writer has included *Bride of the Wind* (2001, directed by Bruce Beresford), a biographical portrait of Alma Mahler, her artistic life, and her relationship as wife/muse of the great composer Gustav Mahler.

About Montemayor Press

Montemayor Press is an independent publisher of literature for children and adults. To learn more about our books, visit

www.MontemayorPress.com

or write for a catalogue at:

Montemayor Press

P. O. Box 546

Montpelier, VT 05601